Too Deep
The Sequel

Michael J. Avery

Table of Contents

1

Present Time

"Happy birthday to you, happy birthday to you, happy birthday, dear Sarah, happy birthday to you!" Everyone sang at the table, including the wait-staff and hostess, before the guest of honor took a moment of reflection on her special day. After making a wish, followed by a wink at Morty, all eighteen candles on the cake were quickly extinguished with one breath. A polite round of applause followed, then Lucile inquired as to her special inclination.

"If I tell you, then it won't come true," she answered. Slices of the beautifully decorated cake were distributed to each guest around the table. Sarah could not be bothered with such ceremony and instead began to open her presents with great ardor. The gifts from her parents were quite beautiful. First a white, long-sleeved turtleneck sweater made of cashmere was unwrapped. An ecstatic squeal of delight was released as she massaged the soft fabric against her cheek. Also inside the box was a black leather skirt that, when displayed, solicited oohs and ahhs from everyone in the party.

Bart and Ethyl were quite generous with their offering of a black leather jacket which perfectly matched the skirt. Sarah was sure to thank each of the guests with an embrace of genuine affection before donning her new coat. Morty's gift was saved as the last to be opened. Although it was the smallest of all the offerings, it commanded the most attention. The jewelry box lid was then slowly raised with distinct intention.

With her eyes wide open, a genuine expression of joy beamed, as those same eyes began to water with delight. Inside the modest cardboard carton lay a heart shaped pendant made of gold, accentuated with a small diamond in the center. Tears streamed down her cheeks, prompting the young lady to jump out of her seat, race around the table, and nearly topple Morty over as she landed in his lap while he sat in his chair.

Such an audacious display was not entirely lost on the group, and Sarah showed no apparent concern, nor did she make any attempt to contain her elation through a very public display of affection. The young man, although somewhat astonished, obliged her for a moment before prompting her to demonstrate some level of restraint. At her urging, Morty secured the trinket around Sarah's neck.

Bart and Ted smiled while the mothers showed their approval by clapping their hands with appreciation. Ted then announced for the benefit of the entire group to hear, "Don't get any ideas about stealing the heart of my little girl, Morty."

"I think you may be a little too late for that announcement," returned Lucile. "Your little girl is growing up, Papa." Morty seemed a little uncomfortable with such a display of affection in front of all the parents, but it was also quite obvious that Sarah could not care less. Ted ordered another round of drinks as Sarah returned to her seat with a restored composure to a more subdued level.

Much had happened to this young couple over the course of the prior year. They had grown so much closer since their first date at the winter formal some nine months earlier. Sarah was new to discover an unbridled freedom from the juvenile trappings which she had felt while attending high school. New experiences presented new emotions, and most everything involved Morty, who was never far away when she needed him. No longer did she identify as a child, or subscribe to any implied obligation to demonstrate restraint with regards to her evolving sexuality. Feelings of endearment progressively deepened, and by all accounts were mutual between the young couple.

As the celebration wound down to a close, there was an air of restlessness to the young lady of honor. She was quite finished with the formal celebration and longed to spend a little time with Morty in private. Sarah bid farewell to her parents in the parking lot of the restaurant, and opted instead to ride with the Thorton family back to their house in Stillwater. The two sat close together in the back seat of the car, but always under the watchful eye of Bart through the rear view mirror. No sooner had they arrived, the young couple parted company from his parents to enjoy a more intimate stroll in the comfort of the late summer evening. A full moon rising from the east began to cast light into the fading sky. Her delicate fingers nervously wriggled the pendant on the necklace when she opened conversation.

"You know, Morty, I'm eighteen now, and I've been thinking a lot about us." She held his arm firmly as they walked. "I'm ready to take our relationship to the next level. I want you to make sweet love to me." She grasped at his arm even tighter. "I don't feel there is a need for us to wait any longer. We've been more than good for a long time, and now, I want us to be just a little bit bad. It's not like we haven't come close, I would guess somewhere between second and third base would be the appropriate terminology. It's time for you to hit a home run!" Under the disguise of a nervous smile, she silently waited for a response.

"I want you too, Sarah, and I'm sure it's going to happen soon," he answered. "I'll admit, I'm more than a little nervous. What if I do it wrong? What if I hurt you? What if you get pregnant?" An underlying anxiety was apparent in his tone.

"Oh, Morty, settle down. You're getting yourself all worked up over nothing. Let's break down all of your concerns. First, this sort of thing must come naturally or we would not be here. Second, I've felt the bulge in your jeans. No offense, but I think I'll be alright. And finally, we will take every precaution possible with all resources available. Don't worry, it's going to be fine."

"I want it to be better than fine. I want it to be the best ever!"

"Well, I'll make a deal with you. Let's say, if it's not the best, then we'll practice more until we get it right." She stopped walking and stood in front of him. With her arms wrapped around his waist she continued, "I'll go to the women's clinic next week and get started on the preparations. I bet they even give out condoms there, too. You can study up on your technique. Don't you have any friends with those kinds of movies that you can watch, you know, for research purposes?"

"I think Benny has some movies like that. I'll check with him the next time we talk." He drew Sarah closer and shared a gentle kiss. "Until then, we'll just have to feel our way through it." He lightly grasped her rear end from around her back with both hands and gave it a squeeze. They continued their walk until reaching Sarah's house.

"I want you to call Benny soon and ask him about the movies. I have to go with my parents tomorrow to see my grandparents, so that would be a good time for you to visit him. Also, I have to go out to the college on Monday and buy my textbooks for this semester. Is there any chance you could come with me?"

"I can't," he said with disappointment. "I'm in clinic until four o'clock. I'll be out there on Wednesday if you want me to go book shopping with you at that time."

"Wednesday's too late. I'll need to go soon if I want to get used books." With one more passionate kiss, she withdrew by tickling his lips with her tongue, and they parted company for the evening. Morty returned home, consumed in thought. Although they had yet to verbalize the word 'love' to each other with regards to their shared feelings, the maturation and evolution of their relationship would lead them down that inevitable path toward such a destination. Soon that bridge would have to be crossed, and he knew it.

Ethyl and Bart prepared for sleep. In her pajamas and housecoat, she greeted her youngest son with a warm, motherly embrace when he entered the house.

"That was quite the display the two of you put on tonight at dinner." A firm hold of his shoulders insured he would not leave while she spoke. "You know, honey, the Finks are getting just a little concerned, and I must say, and I don't blame them.

4

You two have become quite an item over this past summer." There was a short pause before she continued. "We just worry that things between the two of you may be moving a little too fast."

"Is this the sex speech?" asked Morty. "I thought Dad was supposed to give me the speech." An uncomfortable expression crossed her face.

"You're right; let me get your father." Bart was then beckoned from the den by her call. When he arrived, Ethyl leaned toward him to whisper quietly in his ear. Bart grimaced, and then turned his attention to his son.

"Morty, it's like this, Son, when a man and a women get together, certain feelings can happen. These feelings can lead to certain acts. Those acts can lead to babies. Do you get my drift?" Morty nodded his head. "If I find out you're committing certain acts with Sarah, I'll string you up by your short and curlies. Do I make myself clear?" Again Morty nodded. "Good." Bart turned to Ethyl. "Am I done here?" Ethyl sighed, shook her head, and dismissed him from the room with a wave of her hand.

"What your father is trying to say is, we love you both very much and want only the best for the two of you. All we ask is that you don't rush into anything that could affect your, or her chance at a simple, uncomplicated college education. Sarah is an only child, and her parents just want to see her graduate from college. After that, you two can do whatever you want. Morty smiled at his mom and then gave her a comforting embrace.

"Don't worry, Mom. Sarah and I both know what's important, and neither of us want to do anything that could jeopardize our dreams for the future. I know we have become quite fond of each other, but trust me, we work very hard to keep all of that in check."

"Thank you, sweetheart. I know you're a good boy." She pinched his cheek as she spoke. "Be a doll and take out the garbage so the house doesn't stink in the morning."

5

Morty collected the trash and walked it outside to the large metal cans by the garage. The bags were then placed inside, and the lid was fitted tightly to the top. A tight seal would keep feral and stray critters from dumping out the refuse on the ground and rummage through the discarded food during the night, which would make for quite a nasty mess. Once back in the house, Morty placed a call to Benny on the telephone.

It was the harvest season for the grapes at the winery, and Benny was a very busy young man. He worked ten to twelve hours each day, with a start before sunrise in the vineyards. There he made sure the collection of the product went smoothly, and then spent the bulk of the evening hours hauling the berries back to the main processing building for cleaning and de-stemming. As the grandson of the company's owner and founder, he took his responsibilities very seriously. Benny was at home to enjoy a rare evening away from the winery, just watching television when he answered the telephone.

"Hello."

"Hey, Benny. It's Morty. What are you up to tonight?"

"Not much, just relaxing with an ice cold drink. What are you up to?" Benny asked.

"Nothing. I just returned to the house from Sarah's birthday dinner. There's nothing like spending the evening with all of the parents, together at one time."

"Yea, I can see your point," he answered. "How are you two kids doing these days?"

"Pretty good, actually. Probably better than I would have ever expected, but a guy has to get out with his buddy sometime. What are you doing tomorrow?"

"I'm not sure. I was thinking about getting out of town for the day, maybe spend some time at the coast before winter sets in. How was the dinner?"

"It was nice, you know, with the presents and all. That reminds me, I need to ask you a favor." Morty continued with slight reservation, "Do you have any of those adult kind of movies at your house?" The question caught Benny a bit by surprise.

"When you say adult movies, do you mean those that use profanity?"

"Not exactly," answered Morty. "I was thinking more along the line of how babies are made."

"Well, that's an odd question," he answered. "Why would you ask such a thing? Is there trouble between you and Sarah?"

"No, not at all," replied Morty. "We were thinking that it's time to take our relationship to the next level, and I want to be ready when it happens. I figure it couldn't hurt to do some research before the magic moment arrives." Morty's uneasiness was obvious, so Benny tried to have a little fun with his friend.

"I knew that the time would come when I would need to sit you down for a little talk, I just didn't think it would be this soon. You're growing up so fast. Let me see, where do I start? I know; Morton, there comes a time when a young man, such as yourself, begins to take notice of young ladies, such as Sarah. The young man will begin to have strange feelings inside, like none that he has ever felt before. Then, someday, the two of you will want to discover new and exciting things together, and to do things that you have never done before." Benny struggled to suppress the urge to laugh as he spoke. "Then one day, for some unknown reason, the two of you will want to wrestle each other without wearing any clothes."

"OK, funny guy. Are you done yet?" Morty asked.

"She just turned eighteen, right? Man, you two don't waste any time. Yea, I have some movies that can help. What are you doing tomorrow?"

"I have to cut the lawn. After that, I should be free for the afternoon." Morty answered.

"Great! Come over to my house when you're done and I'll let you do a little research. You're a bright kid, so I figure you'll catch on fast. On second thought, maybe you should take lots of notes. Afterward, maybe we can go fishing out at the creek."

"That sounds good. I'll see you tomorrow, Benny." Morty hung up the phone and remained in his room for the remainder of the evening, to catch up on some unfinished schoolwork.

A large harvest moon illuminated an otherwise darkened sky, casting shadows from the tall trees lining the water's edge. Bountiful sounds of nature rang out in full throat to echo across the span of the creek. Chirpings of the combined efforts of a million crickets created a constant hum, only to be periodically broken by the baying of numerous bullfrogs who jostled for an advantageous position amongst all their male contenders in the quest for propagation. A warm, dry evening air made conditions ideal for the cycle of nature to begin anew. As some creatures entered into life, others feasted on the abundant new sources of sustenance that drifted on the breeze, trekked quietly atop the earth, and swam randomly within the waterway.

Nestled deep within the reeds and partially submerged roots of old growth trees along the edge of the waterway, a clump of small, black eggs encased within an opaque gelatin substance floated atop the shallow water, and began to show early signs of life. A transition into an embryonic state was obvious with the relentless movement, until the minute creatures broke through to escape into the current.

These newly hatched tadpoles, arguably one of the smallest living multicellular entities to enter the environment, were not typical. As vulnerable as they seemed, these particular pollywogs exhibited a distinctly aggressive behavior. Any such defenseless newborns would normally seek immediate refuge within the shallow waters, to hide between rocks and crevices along the riverbed. These particular tadpoles made their way directly into the river's current, as if to invite, or even challenge any usual threat that might otherwise enjoy a higher position on the food chain.

Thousands of such offspring dispersed, along with the countless other hatchlings of numerous species to provide a buffet of delicacies for the assembled masses. Of the multitude of tadpoles to hatch, a select few would ultimately survive to develop into adult frogs. Most of those would be consumed by birds, or animals, or even people. Given their sheer numbers, the odds that some would persevere to spawn a new generation were considerably high.

The horrific events of the prior spring were all but forgotten. Tragedies associated with the loss of life had been waved off with little more than convenient excuses, or mere theories based on opinions derived from what little evidence was made available, instead of definitive answers. Morty knew in his heart what had happened. He was there to witness the huge aquatic beast that nearly took his own life, as well. It was impossible for him to forget the fear that he felt while confronting the enormous amphibious creature. Benny was the only one to share in that information, and yet even he voiced occasional skepticism, but always stayed loyal to his best friend. Trepidation for a repeat of those occurrences weighed heavily on Morty's mind, and any incidents to happen near Grizzly Creek would surely spark his interest and concern. He felt confident that the monster which he haplessly helped to create had been destroyed, but he longed to be certain.

Inside an old shoebox, well-hidden on the floor of his bedroom closet is where he kept the paper clippings of the articles saved from the Mercy Gulch Gazette. Reports that detailed the horrific deaths of Bobby Tilson, a young student out for a moonlit swim; George Stalin, the retired custodian who went missing while alone on a fishing trip; and finally Roger Cross, the owner of a mineral processing quarry along the banks of the creek. All of those investigations, which ultimately failed to identify a definitive cause or perpetrator, were coupled with the vague and empty explanations given by the authorities. All this did next to nothing to answer the pertinent questions posed by those unfortunate events. The truth to those unsolved investigations would have to come at a later date, if ever.

Sarah's physical and spiritual metamorphoses were a welcomed distraction for Morty. With the shedding of her childhood veil, womanly wings unfurled, and her soul prepared to take flight. An awakening was in place; a birth of awareness; an insatiable thirst for enlightenment. His was the nectar of life that she so longed to taste, as an elevated level of reverence flowed within her veins. With a focus placed squarely on Morty, such enthusiasm would not be curtailed. No longer would she play the role of a hapless victim of circumstance, a mere passenger on these adventurous and unscripted travels through life. Now, she wished to take total control of those new feelings of empowerment, to place her squarely in the proverbial driver's seat, both hands tightly gripping the steering wheel, and the accelerator pedal pressed firmly against the floor.

Morty recognized his good fortune to bear witness to this development, made obvious by the surge in confidence Sarah displayed. Rarely though, at times he silently pined for the memory of the timid young damsel.

Such a change could prove to be advantageous in his quest of transition to manhood. There could not possibly be a more willing participant, dedicated and loyal, found in this or any other lifetime. Recent displays of her infatuation were intoxicating to his spirit, and ushered a call to awaken the little man inside.

2

Dinner and a Movie

Morty awoke early in the morning to satisfy the landscaping obligations. Conversation with his father in the garage was brief, while a bag of golf clubs was loaded into the trunk of the car. Bart then backed from the driveway and departed for the golf course. Ethyl appeared just as Morty finished with the edging portion of the lawn duties. A plastic tumbler of iced tea, complete with a decorative bright yellow slice of lemon attached to the rim of the cup was offered for refreshment.

"What do you have planned for today, sweetheart?" asked Ethyl, with a detectable tone of enthusiasm.

"I'm going over to Benny's after I finish here," replied Morty. "He's been working too much lately and needs a little distraction." A look of stifled disappointment from Ethyl ensued.

"I guess I'll just have to go to lunch by myself," she said sadly. "Unless, of course, you and Benny would like to go to lunch with me. I'll pick up the check." Morty detected a certain level of desperation in the tone of her voice.

"I tell you what, after I finish with the yard, I'll call Benny and have him meet us at the Golden Mist Restaurant. I should be ready to go in about an hour." Ethyl's mood brightened and she hugged her son in appreciation.

"I had better start getting ready." She walked briskly into the house. Morty interrupted his chore to follow her inside. A telephone call to Benny was placed to inform him of the change in their afternoon plans. Benny was happy to oblige, as he had not seen Ethyl for quite some time, and welcomed the opportunity for a visit. With the yard work complete, Morty returned the gardening equipment to the storage, and entered the house to shower and dress. Ethyl busied herself by tending to the decorative potted plants in the large garden window in the kitchen to pass the time.

Morty insisted that he drive in his own car, as the plans made earlier called for the boys to leave the restaurant for Benny's house after the meal. They all gathered at the entrance of the Asian themed eatery. Benny, gracious as always, greeted Ethyl in a most fictitious manner, almost to the point of being humorously sarcastic.

"Mrs. Thorton, such a pleasure to see you. I can't believe how young you look. Are you doing something different with your hair?" Benny mused, as he bowed down to kiss the back of her hand. "And young Master Morton, why you get so much bigger every time I see you." He reached over and mussed Morty's hair with his hand.

"Is there any wonder why I can't invite you anywhere?" Morty said in protest.

"Now, Morty, that's not true!" Ethyl replied scornfully. "It's always nice to see you, too, Benny. How are things at the winery?

"Things are going quite well, thank you," he answered. "There is a bumper crop of grapes in the vineyards, and with the recent expansion at the winery, we should have a wonderful year, indeed." The party then entered the restaurant and stood patiently at the counter near the cash register. "I would love to bring you a bottle of our finest aged Cabernet."

"That sounds delightful! I would absolutely love a bottle." Ethyl returned, and quietly clapped her hands with glee. "How long has it been aged?"

"At least a week that I know about. That's when I stacked the barrels with a forklift." Benny's answer had all in the group laughing. They were seated soon after, and menus were handed out around the table. Once everyone had been

12

greeted by the waiter, each requested a glass of water prior to placing their food orders.

"Morty tells me you are working an incredible amount of hours at the winery," Ethyl stated. "Does that leave you much time for other things, like girls?"

Morty held the glass to his mouth, but choked on the water after hearing his mother's question. Benny smiled and then replied, "No, I'm afraid not. I'm really not interested in getting too serious at this time." He stopped to take a drink from his glass of water. "What I'm really looking for is a mature woman, one who understands the demands of work and family. Someone much like yourself." He smiled at Ethyl as he spoke. Morty's reaction was a little less subtle as he again choked, and water was spit from his mouth, but was caught in a napkin before it could reach the table.

"Oh, Benny," she answered. "Another time, another place, who knows, but I do appreciate the thought. You are just absolutely darling." Ethyl beamed, flattered with the idea of unsolicited admiration, disingenuous as it was. Her son, by contrast, was quickly losing interest in such subjects of conversation.

"Can we talk about something else, please!" he pleaded.

"Of course. Where are my manners?" Benny seemed to enjoy the level of frustration displayed by his friend. The subject was changed, and caught Morty completely by surprise. "I hear that you and the young Miss Sarah Fink have become quite the item these days. How's that going for you, Morty?" That statement prompted Morty to again gag on the water in his mouth. Benny's amusement was obvious. This time, he was unable to catch the water as it exited his mouth and landed on the table setting. Ethyl handed him a napkin to wipe the expressed fluid from his chin. After a moment to compose himself, his throat was sufficiently cleared before an attempt was made to answer the question. His next words were chosen very carefully.

"Sarah and I are doing quite well. Our relationship, which may appear to be quite serious from an uninformed

13

perspective, is actually just a wonderful friendship of mutual respect and admiration. If there were any possible future plans, those would have to wait until after college is complete." With a short pause for reflection, Ethyl and Benny both retched, expelling water from their mouths after hearing the statement. This attracted the attention of the waiter and prompted a return trip to the table.

"Sum ting wong?" he asked through a very heavy Asian accent. Everyone at the table worked to achieve a higher level of composure and act more appropriately.

Meal orders were placed before the menus were collected from the group. Although they found humor with the waiter's pronunciation, all managed to disguise their amusement and remain respectful. Conversation diverted from the more personal level to a lighter one as the food began to arrive at the table. Of course, Ethyl inquired as to the health and well-being of his extended family, and Benny returned in kind with matters that involved the Thorton clan. With the meal complete, all agreed it was quite delicious and satisfying. Benny made a valiant effort to pick up the check, but Ethyl would not allow that to happen. The remaining food was collected, boxed, and then returned to the table. Ethyl graciously thanked her company for a most enjoyable afternoon, and insisted that Benny take the remaining food home for later. The boys bid farewell to her from the parking lot once they had escorted her to the car.

Morty followed Benny as they drove to his house. The two walked to the front door as Benny's dog, Mat, rested within the shade-covered porch, away from the warmth of the afternoon sun. There, the matted mutt was treated to some of the leftover food from lunch. Mat seemed to enjoy the sauce so much that he even ate all of the broccoli. Morty entered the house and sat on the couch, as Benny excused himself from the room to retrieve the video cassette taped movies that Morty requested earlier for review.

"Now, I've tried to set these up as a quick study guide," stated Benny. "Our first lesson will be the art of undressing. It is important to remember the role that titillation plays in the act of

14

seduction." The television set and video cassette player were both powered on. As the picture on the screen illuminated, Benny inserted the cassette tape. A small writing pad and pen were tossed over to Morty. "You might want to take some notes."

The player was activated, and the image on the screen quickly changed to that of young and attractive couple as they hiked along a dirt trail leading to a beautiful river, on a sun filled afternoon. They carried with them a wicker basket and a folded plaid blanket. Once they found an ideal spot, the blanket was spread out and laid on a small patch of grass along the sandy bank that framed the water's edge. They appeared to be well isolated, far from any prying eyes, to enjoy an intimate picnic lunch. During the meal, a bottle of wine was exhausted, and not long afterward the young couple began to playfully toy with each other.

This quickly escalated to a much more passionate level of kissing and petting. His hands tirelessly began to explore her body. An expression of encouragement in the form of her smile gave him all the license necessary to continue. With a heightened level of awareness, there was an obvious, but not stated point of consent, as her eyes closed and her body wilted. Physical and emotional submission answered his advances. Benny then stopped the tape for review.

"OK, let's take a minute to discuss what we have observed to this point," said Benny. "As you can see from the movie, all of this guy's movements were fluid. There was no wasted energy in the effort. If you watched closely, you would have seen that once he began to kiss her neck, her body became limp, and her head tilted back, and her eyes closed. This is exactly what you want to see. He has now reached the point of no return. If she resists, he must stop. If she consents, like this young lady did, then consider this a green flag, and they're now off to the races! This is the pinnacle, for if you stop now without provocation, she'll get upset because you're an idiot."

Benny rewound the tape to again demonstrate the come-hither expression displayed by the actress as she succumbed to his advances. Morty quickly jotted down a couple of Benny's talking points while the tape was stopped and removed from the player. A second tape was then inserted into the device. Morty used the lull in the lecture to quiz his instructor.

"So, if you know so much about women and romance, how come you don't have a steady girlfriend?"

"Because, I don't want one," Benny was quick to answer. "But that doesn't mean I don't get my fair share of encounters. You have no idea how many lonely women work down at the winery. Most of those girls have been through so much crap that they don't want a regular boyfriend; they just want some occasional attention. I think it may have something to do with their monthly cycles. The best part is, I don't have to take them out to dinner, or buy any gifts, or nothing. Hell, they just stop by here on their way home from work." Morty listened studiously to every word, and smiled with envy. "Enough of that, let's move on to our next lesson." The tape was then cued to play.

The scene began with two very lovely young ladies relaxing outside by a swimming pool, while they enjoyed a beautiful summer's day in the bright sunshine. At ease, they indulged with cocktails along with freshly sliced fruit, and dressed in very revealing swim attire, soaking up the sun atop their matching chaise lounge chairs.

The action heats up as one of the ladies begins to spread tanning oil to the exposed areas of her skin. As she progressively applies the product atop her chest, a non-verbal decision is made to remove the upper portion of her garment, most likely in favor of a tan without any lines caused by the fabric. The second young lady follows suit, but only after a thorough scan of the area to insure their privacy. Soon, the girls were rubbing and caressing each other with delicate but determined enthusiasm, as they continued to apply generous amounts of oil. With their glistening bodies shimmering in the blazing sun, they alternated postures to allow each girl the opportunity to glide against the torso of her partner. Benny again stopped the tape for a quick analysis.

"OK, now we will watch the part you really need to learn. This is a great example of how to give pleasure to a female. I just added the first part because it's freaking beautiful!" He engaged the button to restart the movie.

Moaning soon emanated from each woman as she received a most personal act of attention. The noises were low at first, but rose to a much higher level, one usually associated with childbirth. Such a boisterous display could easily give the perception that the acting might be disingenuous or even deliberate.

The camera work was remarkable. Such professional angles allowed a focus on the anatomy so clear and close that Morty found himself leaning forward in his seat while the events played out on the television screen. Benny again stopped the tape.

"Just a word to the wise, try to keep any substances away from her happy spot. All of that stuff has a bitter taste to it, and can burn if you get it into your eyes. I'm just letting you know, and that goes for lubricants, body paints, and anything else that might find its way down there."

"What does she taste like?" Morty asked. Benny hesitated for just a moment before answering.

"Well, it's hard to say. It can vary between heaven and hell. When I find a good one, giving gratification is easy. Some guys hate it, while others can't get enough of it. It's really about your personal preferences."

The movie resumed without further interruption, to crescendo when the actress erupted in what could only be described as complete sensual bliss. The cassette player was again stopped.

"OK, now you know how to make a girl happy. Next we'll move on to what she can do to make you happy." The tape was promptly removed, and then replaced by yet another into the machine. Again the player was cued to a preselected scene depicting a passionate encounter between a young man and woman.

While coupling, he gently moved forward and then relaxed back. This process was repeated continuously with unpredictable changes in speed and rhythm. Much like the previously viewed encounters, excessive noises were generated from the actors, and seemed somewhat inauthentic until the act was complete. Benny again halted the movie in the player.

"A word to the wise, girls don't always care for that last part. It's commonly referred to as the 'money shot' and is intended to add effect for the movie. Until you get to know her particular fetishes, I recommend you don't try that one." Benny removed the last tape from the player. "Now, you should have a pretty good idea of what is affectionately known as that crazy little thing called love. What we have covered here today was the missionary position and oral copulation, which is also referred to as sodomy by most preachers. There are so many more positions that frankly, we don't have time to go over right now. I think this is a good start, and any further research can be obtained on your own time. Just a little advice; if you want to make her happy, then you should focus on giving her oral pleasure until she climaxes, and then…"

Morty interrupted, "Alright, I get all of that, but when does she give me oral?"

"Whenever she wants, but only until the honeymoon, then it's all over." With that, Benny ended the session by collecting all of the cassettes. "Remember, the woman's needs always come first, or she had better come twice." The cartridges were then returned to the storage cabinet under the television set before the pair prepared themselves for an evening of fishing.

The necessary angling equipment for the upcoming fishing expedition was loaded into the bed of Benny's truck before they departed the house and drove to the bait shop. A single day's fishing license was purchased by Morty, to remain legal and avoid any potential trouble with the game wardens, while Benny paid for the fresh fishing bait and carbonated drinks. They drove out to the creek, adjacent to the bridge near the town of Crescent and parked the truck. A moment was taken to peer out over the water, which precipitated an eerie sense of déjà vu for Morty. This was this very location that George Stalin had mysteriously lost his life just six months earlier, under highly suspicious circumstances. An immediate electric-like current trembled through his body.

The sun retreated behind the uppermost branches along a line of tall oak trees as the pair descended down the steep embankment trail, and to a small clearing near the water's edge. With ambient light fading quickly, the boys set the fishing gear down on a small patch of grass just off the bank of the creek. Benny lit the mantle of the kerosene lantern and set the flame height before the handle was hooked to a nearby tree branch. Care was taken to place it just far enough away to discourage any biting insects from bother. The nylon lines on the poles were straightened and the bait carton retrieved from the food cooler. Plump worms were unearthed from the soil that filled the small Styrofoam container and were attached to the barbed hook at the end of the fishing line. Benny was the first to cast his line into the water. Within a minute, he had the first strike of the night.

"Whoa! Did you see that? That hit nearly took my fishing pole right out of my hand!" The battle against the fish continued with alternating motions to the fishing pole, back and forth, while slowly reeling in the line. Holding constant tension against the struggling creature, the fight began to wane. Morty finished with the preparation to his baited hook before scanning the area for an open spot of water to cast his line into the current. Benny's fish had put on quite a display prior to succumbing to fatigue while being brought into the shore. Hoisting it from the water, Benny was quite surprised when he realized how small the creature was in comparison to the fight it exhibited.

"Wow! He sure felt a lot bigger on the line. It can't be more than a couple of pounds at best."

With much disappointment, Benny released the juvenile catch from the hook and returned to the water. It was a small, striped bass with a distinctively aggressive attitude, in so that it appeared to attempt a strike at its captor, all while in the process of being released. "Well, if that isn't the darnedest thing. I swear, this little guy is trying to get at me."

One sharp slap to the surface of the water startled all the surrounding critters into a moment of silence. A stiff breeze made a light clapping sound through the leaves of the autumn trees. After the setting of the sun, the wind diminished, and the sounds of nature resumed.

Morty landed his first strike of the evening with a hit so strong it seemed to more closely match that of an eight to ten pound specimen hell bent on escaping capture from the nylon monofilament rein. The fishing pole arched so close to the point of breaking, that Morty was prompted to release a little extra line and drag from the reel to ease the tension, and allow the fish to more easily exhaust by swimming for a little while longer. With hardly any noticeable decline in the fight, he persuaded this small adversary to the creek's edge, and then out of the water. Although the fish was again quite small in size, the effort was more than expected for such a nominal prize.

As soon as the barbed end of the hook was removed from the throat of the feisty critter, it was returned to the watery habitat. This exercise was repeated in nearly a scheduled manner for the next three hours. The last fish Benny landed was the biggest of the night. It took all of the skill and finesse he could muster to encourage the fish to the shore without damaging the line or pole. This fish was larger than the rest, and fought gallantly. At first glance, the size was rather impressive, and looked to weigh about ten pounds. Benny announced with pride that this one would be taken home. It was then placed within the cooler, and submerged in ice to keep the kill fresh.

A biting chill from the evening air increased over time. This was made obvious through a thin mist generated with each exhaled breath. Both anglers felt content to declare that it had been a good outing, worthy of their efforts, and collected the gear. During the drive back to Benny's house, a distinct banging noise came from the back of the truck and drew their attention. The unsecured cooler was seen sliding across the bed, as it bounced from side to side. When they reached Benny's house, the tackle was removed along with the ice chest and placed on the front lawn prior to entering. The top of the chest was propped opened to allow Benny to look at the fish. It continued to squirm, even though over an hour's time had passed since it had been initially placed within. It still showed signs of life, a lot of life, and should have perished with the passing of such time.

The catch was brought into the house and carefully removed from the cooler. Benny struggled to hold it down firmly against the cutting board as he proceeded to slice the creature's soft white underbelly open with a knife. The internal organs were then removed and studied. The stomach and intestinal tract wiggled on top of the wooden surface, completely free of the host. When the stomach was cut open, multiple black tadpoles were released from their confinement and moved in an effort to escape. Benny grabbed a meat mallet from the utensil drawer to strike at the small creatures, pounding them continuously until complete annihilation was achieved. The remains were closely examined before being discarded into the trash can. Next, the head and tail were removed with a knife. Benny took the opportunity for a little levity when he placed the index and middle fingers of his right hand deeply into the raw flesh of the fish. He then raised his hand to Morty.

"Smell my fingers!" Morty swiped to keep Benny's hand from reaching his face.

"You're not really going to eat that, are you?" Benny headed Morty's warning, and stopped for a moment to think about the possible ill effects that could come from consumption.

"No; you're right. There's definitely something wrong with this fish." He scraped all of the remaining flesh into the garbage can with the carving knife and then closed the lid. Morty walked into the living room and turned on the television set. The large knob was tuned to scan the channels until stopping on the evening news telecast.

The lead-in headline story of the program centered on the odd, recent occurrences taking place around Grizzly Creek.

Numerous reports documented the unusual behaviors of wild and domestic animals in the vicinity of the waterway. Such stories spanned along the creek from Mercy Gulch to Emery Lake. Local emergency services providers detailed the ongoing treatment of unnamed people stricken with what appeared to be some unknown form of food poisoning.

Doctor Chandler, the medical Chief of Staff at Our Lady of Miraculous Recovery Hospital, gave an interview to station correspondent Gabby Jargon during the aired segment.

"Doctor Chandler, what is causing all the recent, strange behaviors of people and animals seen in the county?" She pushed the microphone at his face to extort a response.

"Honestly, we don't know. I can only comment on the treatment of the people that have presented for care. We here at the hospital, and all the surrounding local hospitals and clinics have documented numerous patient complaints of those who have displayed erratic, atypical behaviors. The most likely causes points to a distinct correlation between the eating of any of the potential food sources taken from the creek, and the subsequent changes to behaviors after ingestion. We have recently admitted numerous patients to the hospital over the past two weeks, all displaying very similar changes with regards to their mental capacities. Those affected display a certain stupor, or trance-like state that could lead to traumatic accidents caused by a lapse in cognitive thinking. The good news is, these effects appear to be transient in nature, and following a successful courses of I.V. antibiotic therapies and hydration, all those affected individuals have returned to a full level of recovery with no permanent disabilities identified."

Ms. Jargon continued with her aggressive line of questioning. "We are receiving unconfirmed reports that there have been teenagers and young adults who have begun to seek out these rumored mind altering sources as a means of recreation. Have you witnessed any such behavior during your treatments at the hospital?" Ms. Jargon again returned the microphone to the doctor.

"Unfortunately, it seems that any time there is a substance with the ability to alter one's mindset, that information is quickly shared with those who also seek out such sources. We see this every day, whether it's a controlled substances, or those of a more organic nature, people will attempt to abuse such resources for personal entertainment purposes. We are asking for the public's help in isolating the source, and lend aid to our collaborative efforts to stop the spread of this problem. We have obtained blood and tissue samples collected from infected individuals and submitted them to the state pathology lab for a detailed analysis. As there are no known native species that possess psychoactive bufotoxins, this may, in fact, represent the introduction of an alien species to the habitat. Substances derived from the excretions of these creatures are believed to be responsible, and that is the main focus of our investigation. We will continue to work in tandem with local authorities to identify any chemical compound or possible agent that could provide for, or enable these types of anomalies to occur."

The report then moved to an interview with Hank DuTray, the local representative of the state fish and game department. He was the agent supervising the investigation.

"Warden DuTray, can you shed any light on the recent strange occurrences at the creek?" The direction of his response was focused more on the cause rather than the effect.

"I wish I could tell you what is behind all these unusual events. What I can tell you is that we will be exhausting all public resources available to find the source of the problems along the creek. We have begun setting traps and collecting data from all available local wildlife species in order to perform a thorough investigation. We ask for the cooperation of the general public to refrain from interfering with our efforts to collect information, or to fish, gig, or otherwise take or consume any game acquired from the creek, or any adjacent areas of the waterway." Benny commented with regards to the telecast.

"This is so cool. I'm eating that fish." Benny motioned as if he would retrieve the fish from the trash receptacle. Morty felt compelled to intervene.

"Have you lost your mind? If you eat that thing you'll end up in the hospital like those other people." Satisfied with his anticipated reaction from Morty to the idea, he relaxed back into the chair.

"Yea, you're probably right. We've had enough fun for one day, and I have to report to work early tomorrow. Do me a favor and toss this in the garbage can outside, on your way home, so it doesn't stink up my house."

Morty agreed and disposed of the tainted fish during his walk out to the car. On the drive home, he became more distracted with recurrent thoughts of the large mutant killer frog that he had destroyed in the creek earlier that same year, with the help of the disguised explosive that Benny had assembled. He wanted to believe that the recent problems at the creek had nothing to do with that frog, and would eventually resolve naturally without further intervention on his part. He soon found himself back at home, and all those thoughts of river monsters and mutant fish gave way to a much needed rest. After cleaning up and removing his odoriferous clothing to the laundry area of the garage, he retired to his bedroom for the night.

3

Season of Change

Talk of the strange fish began to generate quite a buzz within the general public of the county. Local anglers reported that any fish taken from Grizzly Creek would continue to thrash for hours after being removed from the water. The aggressive nature of the tadpoles extracted from within the stomachs and intestinal tracts of the affected fish gave pause as well, with some of them demonstrating early stages of digestion. With an ominous and quite eerie look to the creatures, the eyes of the captured game were noted to appear sullen and dark, with an almost trance-like stare. The mouths of those affected seem to continuously bite at the air or water, regardless of any purpose or reward. The tail would constantly slap back and forth, with a slow, deliberate motion: not typical of the usual efforts to escape or flee. Local officials began to concentrate their investigative efforts along the creek from just outside of the town of Crescent to the O.I. Gebiah Dam, and the mouth of the river where it flowed into Emery Lake. A photograph of Warden Hank DuTray of the state fish and game department accompanied the article in the local newspaper. The printed message conveyed the same information as that of the televised newscast which had aired the night before and was viewed by Morty at Benny's house.

The weekend arrived in routine fashion, with a cup of coffee to drink while reading the morning paper at the dining room table. Bart, had already departed the house for the golf course, and would remain there for the better part of the morning. Ethyl entered the room and dispensed a motherly kiss to the top of his head, then took a cup from the cabinet and poured herself some coffee.

"What do you have planned for today?" she asked.

"First, I'll do our yard, then go to Sarah's and take care of theirs." A heavy sigh followed. "I really need to find a more consistent way to make money before the winter sets in. After the weather turns cold and the rainy season comes, there'll be no more grass to cut every week."

Ethyl took a portion of the newspaper from Morty and settled into a seat across from him at the table. "You should ask Benny if there are any jobs you can do at the winery. I'm sure there must be something out there for you." She flipped the pages and stopped to read the obituary listings. "Oh, my, it says here that Mrs. Peterson passed away last week." Her expression soured while she continued to read the article. "It was only a month ago when her husband died. It says here that the Petersons were married for seventy-seven years. She must have succumbed to a broken heart." She stopped reading to find her cup and take a drink of coffee. "How romantic is that?"

"A broken heart? How old was she?" Ethyl paused for a moment to perform a quick mental calculation.

"Um, ninety-two years old," she replied.

"That's not a broken heart. That's called congestive heart failure." Ethyl lowered the paper to leer at him from across the table.

"Must you make a joke about something so serious?"

"Come on, Mom; she was ninety-two years old. It's not like they were Romeo and Juliet. They survived droughts, pre-vaccination diseases, a stock market crash, cars without seat belts, and two world wars. I'd say they were some of the luckiest people who ever lived." Ethyl's expression lightened.

"Well, I guess when you look at it that way, it doesn't sound so bad," she said, and flashed a smile at him.

"That's the only way to look at it," he answered. "I better get started on the yards." He finished his coffee and placed his cup in the sink. The morning air was still a little cool, with a slight glistening to the grass from the dew. Morty retrieved the lawn equipment and started with the edging.

Ethyl was leaving the house when she stopped and called out so as to be heard over the noise of the mower while he cut the yard. "I'm going shopping with Lucile and Sarah. Do you need anything from the mall?"

"Nothing that I can think of," he answered. "I'm going over to their house to do that lawn after I have finished here. Will anyone be home to let me in?"

"I'll tell Lucile to leave the side door open to the garage so you can get at the tools." She blew him a kiss from across the yard before entering her car. With a wave, she drove away from the house and out of his view. Morty returned his attention back to his weekly chore. Once he finished in the back yard, he took a short break and entered the house for a drink of juice and a light snack. Bart returned from his morning golf game and entered the house through the garage.

"What's your plan for today?" he asked, as he removed his spiked shoes before entering the kitchen.

"I'm going to the Fink's house to cut their yard," he answered.

"You know, Son, the Finks have you do their yard because they pity you. Now, I'm not trying to be mean intentionally, but you need to start thinking about finding something a little less pathetic to do for money." Morty stood and listened respectfully to his father's speech before seizing the opportunity to defend himself.

"I'm limited in what work I can do because of the number of hours spent at school, and the training that I perform at the hospital. I asked the manager at the hospital about any job opportunities in the evenings or weekends as an orderly, or maybe in housekeeping. Unfortunately, they're not hiring right now. Mom had a good suggestion earlier today, so I'm going to ask Benny if there is any work I can do at the winery to earn some extra money." Pleased with the response, Bart managed a slight grin.

"Well, it sounds like you're on the right track. Good luck with that." He patted Morty on the shoulder, then moved to pass him and continue down the hallway toward his bedroom. Morty cleaned up in the kitchen and finished his task in the yard before leaving the house. He gained access to the Fink's yard equipment stored in the garage by entering through the gate of the fence. He opened the unlocked door at the side of the garage. The switch to the main electric door was activated and opened, which allowed Morty to tend to the front yard. As he neared completion of the task, the women returned home from their day of shopping. No sooner had the car stopped, Sarah leaped out from the back seat and ran to Morty with unbridled excitement.

"Morty, I have great news!" she exclaimed. I got a job at Madame Souris' Boutique!" She bounced up and down before stopping to embrace him. It was then that she realized he was covered in sweat and dust, so she loosened her grip. "I'll be working every weekend, and maybe some evening hours during the holiday season. Isn't this wonderful news?" She could hardly contain her enthusiasm. The mothers approached and participated with the excitement of Sarah's news.

"And she gets an employee discount, so the two of you can do all your birthday and holiday shopping for us there." Although Lucile was the one to make the announcement, Ethyl could not agree more.

"Are you happy for me, Morty?" Sarah asked.

"Of course I am," he replied. "But who's going to help me with the yards?"

"Oh, Morty, you'll be fine without me," she answered, and attempted a hug while trying to avoid contact with his sweat-covered skin. "We'll still have our mornings together." Morty was happy for her, but could not disguise the disappointment of his own anemic economic plight. "It was easy!" she so gleefully continued, "I was at the register and just asked about a job. The manager came out to meet me, asked a few questions, and gave me a job!" She leaped with glee and clapped her hands as she spoke. His response, while more poignant, showed some joyfully restraint.

"That's great! I know you'll do a wonderful job." Morty slowly swept the walkway while he continued to talk. "If you need a letter of recommendation, I would be glad to write one for you." That statement gave Sarah cause to smile. "It's going to be tough to replace you, though," he continued. "I was thinking of marketing this job as 'a pretty young girl cuts your yard' kind of thing. I guess I'll just have to put an ad in the paper for your pretty young replacement. Maybe you could help me with the applicant interviews?" Sarah's demeanor soured immediately.

"I think you'll get along all by yourself just fine!" she said scornfully. "You just need to take your time and don't be in a big hurry. I could even help you in the morning, if we start early." Morty began to transfer the lawn equipment to the rear of the property while Sarah helped to complete the task. As the mothers enjoyed a glass of iced tea under the shade of the awning on the back patio, Sarah changed her clothes for a more casual attire to aid Morty with finishing his chore.

"Do you want to do something tonight?" Sarah asked Morty through a hushed tone, far from their mothers' range of hearing.

"Yea, I do," he answered, "but, I need to go by Benny's house and ask him about a job." She was disappointed with his answer, but had a back-up plan. "Mom, it looks like I'm available for dinner tonight!" Her voice easily carried across the length of the yard.

"OK, honey," returned Lucile. "You should think about getting ready because we're pretty hungry!" Sarah returned her attention back to Morty.

"Speaking of Benny: Did you ever get a chance to research our little thing?" She labored to hide enthusiasm for their delightful little plan of decadence, with a keen eye kept toward their mothers.

"Yea, I learned a lot. I have a pretty good idea what to do, but I don't want to rush, you know."

"I know: Me neither." She answered using a calm and soothing voice. "No pressure or anything, but, my appointment at the clinic is on Wednesday, after school." She then leaned to him and shared a small kiss against his salty lips. After flashing him a most teasing little smile, she dashed into the house to prepare for supper. Morty completed the yardwork and promptly returned the equipment to its proper storage areas. He bid a good evening to the women before leaving for home to call Benny on the telephone.

Once the dirt and sweat had been effectively removed in the shower, he dressed for a casual evening out with his friend.

Conversation between the two centered mostly on the unusual events at the creek, and any correlation there might be to the mutant frog that Benny's efforts helped to destroy about six months earlier. Eventually, Morty worked up enough nerve to request Benny's help to secure a job at the winery. With a slight air of desperation, laced carefully within the shameless solicitation, Benny responded. With a certain degree of confidence, he boasted that could procure for Morty a part time job in a security guard capacity during the weekends. Morty would work the evening shift every Saturday and Sunday, all while retaining opportunities to study for school.

The job would pay well, nearly twice when compared to the minimum wage choices for a typical college student's employment opportunities. He knew this could lead to spending less time with Sarah, and caused some heartache, but knew it to be the responsible thing to do.

The couple planned to enjoy the entire day together on Sunday. Morty arrived at Sarah's house just before eleven o'clock in the morning, and the pair soon drove out to Mercy Gulch, to allow an opportunity for Sarah to submit the appropriate paperwork at Madame Souris' for her employment. After that, a casual lunch date and time spent together with no set plan or obligation. He sat alone at a table in the food court and waited for her, and sipped from a large cup of ice-cold soda pop.

Without warning, Rebecca Branson appeared. She was a former classmate: An attractive young lady who had caused Morty great excitement the year prior. They were partners in the anatomy class during Morty's first semester at the college, and the object of his mental affections during a short spell.

"Hey, Morty! How's it going? I haven't seen you since forever!" Morty flinched with the surprise of the greeting, and nearly dropped his cup. Standing at the opposite end of the table, she motioned toward the open seat at the table across from him. "Mind if I join you?" Without waiting for a response, she sat down. Instantly, he rose up from his seat and stuttered with an attempt to respond.

"Hi, B-Becky. What are you doing here?"

"Oh, I don't know, maybe shopping?" She answered with a dry wit, while motioning toward all the stores that surrounded their table. "Did I catch you at a bad time?" Morty could not help to notice how pretty Becky looked in her skin-tight denim jeans and formfitting blouse. He was sure that Sarah would notice that as well, and she would be returning for him at any moment. "What have you been doing lately?"

"N-Nothing, absolutely nothing," he responded with obvious duress. "I'm just going to school, nothing exciting, no, nothing exciting at all."

"Morty, are you alright?" she continued. "I swear, I haven't seen you this nervous since we went swimming together at the lake house." He was nervous, but this time he wasn't submerged in freezing water.

"Yea, I guess so. How have you been?"

"Jolly good, thank you," she answered with the worst attempt at a British accent that he had ever heard. "I just returned from holiday across the pond, and it was smashing!" They both laughed, which allowed Morty to lower his guard for just a moment.

"Hi, honey. What's so funny?" Sarah announced her arrival with a forceful tap to his back. Her appearance put a shock into Morty that sent his soda cup flying into the air, then crashing to the ground, allowing ice and drink to scatter all over the floor. Morty then scrambled to retrieve the cubes using his hand, and pushed all of waste into the empty cup. "Oh, Morty, you can be so clumsy sometimes." There was an uncomfortable pause in the conversation before Sarah looked at Becky with a quizzical stare. "You know, you look very familiar," Sarah stated, as she pointed at Becky with her middle finger. "Where have I seen you before?" Becky smiled back politely.

"I remember, we met out at the college last spring." You were visiting from the high school, right?" Sarah's response escaped through a labored smile.

"Yes, now I remember. How nice to see you again. "Anyway, let's get going, sweetheart. We have a date for lunch today, and I'm ready." She pulled hard at his shirt in an attempt to quickly whisk him away. "It was great to see you again, Bertha was it?"

"That's Becky. It was nice to see you again, Morty. Maybe I'll see you later. Good bye, Sally!" Becky waved her hand and smiled at the couple while they departed.

"That's Sarah, and yes, good-bye!" Morty was then briskly escorted away from the food court. Well out of Becky's earshot, Sarah slowed her pace and slightly relaxed her grip to his arm. "I can't leave you alone for one minute. Why the heck were you talking to her back there?"

Morty was dumbfounded for an answer, so he merely restated the facts. "I was just waiting for you. I did not invite that conversation. She walked up on me." With conviction, he pleaded his innocence.

"Well, next time just get up and run away. You don't need to be talking to girls like that." The subject was quickly changed to that of a more pressing matter.

"I start working next Saturday. She wants me to be there at one o'clock and work until five o'clock, for training. This shouldn't be too hard. I just need to learn the cash register and how to process credit cards. I will make three dollars and fifty cents per hour, plus a ten percent commission on sales."

They walked down the mall until reaching the Dream River Restaurant, and then proceeded inside to the hostess' podium. After a short wait, the young couple was seated at a table prior to a drink order being taken by the waitress. Sarah flipped opened her menu and scanned down at the variety of choices. Morty studied his menu, too, but struggled to start a conversation that may prove to be difficult.

"Sarah, I have something to tell you, but I don't want you to get upset." Her expression turned deadly serious, drawing her attention away from the menu. "Benny said he thinks he can get me a job at the winery, maybe as a security guard. Sarah chuckled with amusement with the off-guard comment, but quickly composed herself.

"I'm sorry Morty. I didn't mean to laugh." She covered her mouth with a napkin to disguise any sign of amusement.

"What's so funny about that?" He commanded an answer.

"Well, honey, I just don't see you as a security guard." Sarah's tried to smooth him over using a more sweet tone in her voice.

"And why not!" His temper rose.

"You know, I mean, you're more of the..." she struggled to finish the sentence, but found herself committed to a response. "You're more of the superhero type!" Her smile was a bit overdone. "It's like, you appear to be a mild-mannered kind of guy until you spring into action." She motioned with her hands as if to mimic an explosion.

"I can do this," he insisted. "It's not like I'm guarding a bank."

"What are the hours?" she asked. Morty hesitated before responding.

"Saturday and Sunday, three o'clock until eleven thirty, at night." Sarah froze for a moment, took a deep breath, and then continued.

"OK. We can do this. We'll still have our Friday nights, and most of the mornings to spend together on the weekends. My dad is sure going to miss you on Saturdays. He said that he really loves having another guy around the house."

"We can still take care of the yards," returned Morty enthusiastically. "We just won't charge them any money for it. It will be fun, and I'm sure our folks will appreciate it." Sarah smiled more and stressed a little less once the initial shock of the changes to come subsided. They soon found a level of comfort and enjoyed a wonderful meal without any further drama. A hearty cheese burger, stacked high with bacon and other toppings, plus French fries appealed to Morty, while Sarah kept her meal a little lighter with a Cesar salad and fettuccine Alfredo dish.

After the meal, with beautiful weather outside, and the pair not quite ready to end their evening so early, they decided to drive out to the Mercy Gulch Park. A romantic stroll along the paved asphalt path that followed the creek's edge would certainly enhance the date. They held hands as they walked, only stopping occasionally to share a kiss, or some playful banter. Sarah left the trail and stood closer to the water's edge before she turned around and faced him.

"Where do you see us in five years?" she asked. Morty thought deeply before responding.

"That kind of sounds like something you would hear at an interview. Well, let's see, that's a very good question." Under a furrowed brow, he thought quite carefully before submitting an answer. "I can't say exactly where we'll be physically, but I'm absolutely sure that our hearts will be together." She took comfort from his words, made obvious by a smile and slightly tighter grip on his hand.

"I sure hope so. I'm not afraid to say that I have fallen hard for you Morty, so please don't screw this up." They embraced, locked tightly within the arms of the other. Gazing deeply into her eyes, Morty declared his mutual feelings of endearment.

"I have no intention of ever hurting you. I only want to be able to give you the best that life has to offer."

Before they could melt into a kiss, a loud splash echoed from across the shallow waters along the banks of the creek. It startled her and prompted a considerably firmer grasp to the fabric of his shirt. Circular ripples grew and spread slowly atop the surface of the water before fading into the perpetual motion of the current.

Morty's thoughts drifted back to the prior spring season, and his mission of redemption at the creek. He felt confident that the mutant amphibian that he unwittingly helped to create, had been destroyed, but still, he longed for the slightest shred of definitive proof. A cause to the mild disturbance in the water proved similarly elusive with nothing obvious in view. Sarah demanded the return of his attention with a strong pull at the sleeve of his shirt.

"Morty, are you alright? You seem a little distracted."

"No, I'm OK. I think it's time we start heading home. We've had a busy weekend and I've got to be in the clinic tomorrow morning." They returned to the car and ended the evening with a drive back to Stillwater, and a kiss at Sarah's front porch.

4

Like a Dream

Morty's studies at the hospital and at school progressed, and the staff at Our Lady of Miraculous Recovery proved to be very friendly and helpful. Donna Stump, his classmate also assigned to that same radiology department, seemed to thrive within this specific work environment as well. She remained close to the female technologists, and dedicated a considerable amount of her time to training in the mammography discipline, where radiographic imaging of the breast tissues took place. These types of exams were growing in popularity as a medical necessity in preventive medicine, but were performed by the female staff technologists exclusively. Such practices provided the female radiographer with a distinct advantage in the job market. Morty chose to spend his elective time to study in the computerized axial tomography modality, or CAT for short. He was fascinated by the new technology.

The patient is placed in a recumbent position on a long, narrow table. An initial exposure is generated to produce a 'scout' image of the patient. That image would be used to program the parameters of the exam. The patient is then moved through the gantry in ten millimeter increments while the X-ray tube rotated around the patient. Collected data from the radiation detectors transferred information to the computer.

That data was converted to a digital signal and assigned a specific value through interpolation coinciding with the various pixel values based on signal intensity. Calculations performed by the computer enabled the production of a two-dimensional picture. Ultimately, this information would be permanently transferred to a film medium for interpretation and as a permanent part of the medical record for the patient. The technology allowed the physician to virtually dissect a living patient, and visualize the internal organs for evidence of pathology. Such information could be of great benefit in the treatment of the examined patient.

The morning schedules were reserved for the dynamic contrast studies performed daily on patients who were instructed to follow specific dietary restrictions prior to exam, and conducted under the direct supervision of a doctor, occasionally with the aid of fluoroscopy.

Fluoroscopy is live X-ray television where instant images are viewed and captured to study dynamic processes. During a routine exam, a suspension of fluid containing a heavy metal called barium would be introduced into the patient directly within the alimentary canal.

Barium sulfate is a heavy metal compound with a low toxicity level, but a relatively high density, manufactured for medical and industrial applications. In medicine, it is used to visualize structures of the digestive system. Once the fluid has been introduced into the patient, the doctor observes the liquid as it passes through the alimentary tract. Radiographic images are then generated for further analysis of diagnostic pathology. Fluoroscopy allows the physician to view internal organs and their functions as they occur, much like watching a television program.

These types of exams would consume the better part of the morning appointments, as the patients were instructed to refrain from eating or drinking during a specified period of time prior to the exam. The afternoon duties were unique, with tests of a more intravenous nature. These tests called for the patient to be subjected to an iodine-based solution administered directly into the vein, spine, or articulating joint spaces. The high density molecular nature of the liquid makes visualization of vascular structures, spinal cavities, and tendon or ligament maladies visible. The urinary filtering and excretion process is also evaluated utilizing this same type of process. When injected under higher volume and pressure, the arterial segment of the circulatory system is more easily studied and documented.

Morty worked well with the entire staff, and displayed a natural aptitude for the vocation. He seemed to gravitate toward a particular technologist named Rick Fierro, a young man about his same age, who had recently graduated from Mercy Gulch Community College. Rick was fortunate to secure a position at the hospital after the completion of his studies. The two young men enjoyed many of the same interests with regards to professional sports teams and classic automobiles. They would often take lunch together to discuss such matters that are important to men. Morty was issued a meal card by the hospital that allowed him to eat at no cost in the cafeteria, and he in turn was generous to share his good fortune with Rick, in the form of cookies, cake, or whatever sweet confection was available during their shared meal times. Rick in turn would help Morty to better his understanding of the often subtle nuances with respect to the individual personas of the other staff members, or with regard to routine departmental protocol. As part of his studies, four days of the week were mandated in the clinical setting, eight hours a day. Nearly full-time work by most standards. Wednesdays were dedicated on campus, in the classroom, from nine in the morning until four in the afternoon.

Sarah's enrollments would find her busy throughout the week with registrations in classes of English, history, anatomy, and human sexuality studies during her first full semester. Such commitments would leave little time for any intimate social interaction, and the young couple found reinforcement of their feelings for each other through frequent telephone conversations as a way to augment their loss of intimate time together. Even though they possessed and displayed strong feelings toward each other, they had yet to proclaim the highest level of affection through the use of the word 'love' when referencing those types of feelings.

They verbally avoided the subject directly, but frequently expressed their 'love' when describing nearly everything else that brought joy to their lives. It was quite easy for them to confess their love for pizza, or puppies or kittens, and never gave a moment's hesitation to express amorous feelings for the many gifts found in life. It was only difficult to confess their love for each other.

Such a declaration would constitute a major step forward in their relationship, and could result in a monumental change with regard to the family dynamics for both the Thorton and the Fink households, as well. Through admission, the expectations of an exclusive relationship would follow. Morty feared that he may lose touch with his few remaining friends from childhood, with obligations of more time with Sarah's inner circle of family and friends. The reaction of the parents to this revelation would also have to be taken into consideration. To this point, they remained innocent and uncomplicated, although recent developments pointed to a definite change on the horizon.

Morty departed from the school a little earlier than usual on Wednesday afternoon. He feigned illness during the late session and drove his car out to the winery. Benny had made good on his earlier promise of a job, but Morty still needed to submit the necessary paperwork for personal and tax information prior to completion of an orientation. It was there that he would receive the specific task assignment requirements and a thorough tour of the grounds before starting work on Saturday. Plans were already set for an evening out with Sarah on Friday, so this would be his only opportunity to complete the prerequisites mandated for employment.

The job requirements seemed simple: Direct traffic while the employees entered and exited the property during shift changes, aid employees with issues regarding parking, and patrol the grounds in the evening hours for loss-control and surveillance of the company assets. He would be assigned a small, three-wheeled, off-road motorcycle, with large balloon-type tires and a pull-cord starter. This mode of transportation would aid to transverse areas of the property not easily accessed from the paved roads. A small shed structure that measured sixty square feet and located at the main gate would be the designated area in which he would spend a majority of his time while on duty. Inside the office there was a two-way radio for internal communications among the plant supervisors, and a telephone for external contact with the police or any other necessary emergency responders. Wages for the job paid well, as much as twice the established minimum wage, which would be a welcomed change from the meager earnings from all of his prior employment opportunities.

When Friday evening arrived, the young couple greeted each other with honorable enthusiasm on Sarah's front porch prior to their departure. Plans for the evening started with an early casual meal, then to take in a movie at the theater in Mercy Gulch. Sarah burst with energy and expressed playfulness during the entire dinner by exhibiting flirtatious facial expressions through the use of her winking eyes and puckered lips. There was also persistent contact made by her feet after her shoes were removed to massage his calf muscles using just the ends of her toes. With the formality of the meal completed, she coquettishly suggested a slight deviation from the earlier plan. Her idea was for a drive to a more secluded location in a quiet, rural setting of the county. She didn't want to sit in a cold, dark, noisy theater for hours when they could instead find somewhere to relax and enjoy a dark, quiet and romantic location for a private interlude. He readily agreed, and soon they exited the paved road, opting for a short drive along the dusty trail adjacent to an almond orchard along the creek, not far from town.

After the car was parked, the young couple paused to take in the moment. The engine was stopped, and Morty dramatically stretched out, then reached over to her by placing his arm around her shoulder. Outside, the world was hushed, as the muffled sounds of nature nurtured an atmosphere of solitude. Nervous smiles emanated from the pair, and soon neither could contain their excitement for the long anticipated events that were to follow. To complete the mood, Morty set the radio to play at a low volume, which also provided a soft illumination of light from the station indicator dial.

Sarah removed the wad of chewing gum from her mouth and tossed it out of the window. Morty seized the moment by removing the safety belt of the seat to lean toward her direction. Their lips met with a kiss, slowly at first, but soon mounted to a more passionate display of affection. His free hand began to explore the uppermost areas of her petite frame through a

40

delicate gliding motion around her shoulders and neck. Such movements were paced and deliberate, based on the prior tutoring by Benny; not quite seamless to the point of appearing choreographed, even though this was indeed his plan. For so long he fantasized about this very moment, from that night on the beach, after the spring dance, when she declared her intentions for him. Although her body remained rigid, there was no indication of resistance. They were both quite nervous, but in the best of ways, each determined to see this through to a highly anticipated conclusion. Now was the time to take their relationship to the next level and they knew it. They were in too deep, and there would be no turning back.

Morty summoned the courage to slowly open the buttons on her blouse and explore the soft form of the brazier with the palm of his hand. Using gentle motions, he caressed the areas beneath the fabric while the garment was unfastened. With eyes closed, her head sank back, and all the anxious tension from within seemed to leave her body. His efforts became much more fluid, and within moments she was topless. Discarded clothing was tossed into the back seat with attention now focused on the buttons found in the front of her denim pants.

Sarah unleashed her inner animal and began to kiss him with a forceful delicacy, pushing her tongue firmly against his mouth. Breathing turned labored and rapid, and her passion escaladed to a gentle biting of her own lip. Morty pressed his body closer and soon was kissing her neck, just under the edge of her jaw, and worked to remove the remaining garments of her lower regions. She leaned back against the seat, eyes closed, and released a muted moan.

Try as they might to remain focused to their task, neither could ignore the instant illumination of the sky from outside of the car. The light intensified to the point where Morty reluctantly halted his efforts and turned his attention outward.

Both now found themselves shielding their eyes from the blinding glow. Initially Morty feared it could originate from the spotlight of a rancher's truck, as they had parked on private property without prior permission. Worse yet, it could be directed from a vehicle of a more official nature, as in police or game warden, which would bring an end to the evenings activities on a most embarrassing note.

With mounting anxiety, Sarah clutched at Morty, with wrapped arms securely clasped around his neck in a grip so tight that he soon found it difficult to breathe. In need of air, he worked to loosen her grasp and brace for whatever was to follow. An eerie silence ensued as they prepared for what would transpire. No persons appeared, and there was no detectable movement outside of the car. With no indication of immediate danger, Morty turned his attention back to Sarah. He tried in vain to ease her anxiety by disguising any outward signs of his own distress.

There was a palpable energy in the air that caused the small hairs on the back of the neck to stand. No sounds could be heard or uttered, with a noticeable silence to the crickets and other wild creatures. No voices called out. Without any provocation, Morty slowly exited the car to investigate this aerial anomaly. Sarah clutched the loose articles of clothing to her chest and watched intensely from the safety of her seat in the automobile.

"Be careful, Morty." She quietly called out.

The light that originated from above was like none he had ever seen before now. Straining to look straight up at the source, he could barely make out the circular silhouette of a craft that hovered just above the tops of the trees, without making any sound. Morty froze and could do little else but shield his eyes as he stared blankly into the night sky. Sarah's curiosity overtook her fear when she dressed and exited the car to join him at the edge of the fender and watch in utter disbelief.

Then things became fuzzy before everything completely changed. When their senses returned, both he and Sarah were lying supine on a raised illuminated platform. All of their clothing had been removed, with only the heart-shaped pendant necklace Sarah wore remaining on her person. Helplessly they lay, side-by-side, unable to move or communicate with the other.

Through his mental fog, Morty began to visualize the strange outlines of life forms which were completely alien to him, as they stood along the edge of the platform in quiet observation.

These beings carried unusually large heads anchored to shoulders by a freakishly thin neck. Large, round, black eyes sank deeply into those bulbous heads. Their bodies appeared frail and quite small in stature, with long boney arms attached to tiny hands, with three fingerlike projections attached to each one.

Sarah's nude body began to levitate, and rose up just prior to a slow rotation into the prone position. As she hovered directly above him, Morty could now look directly into her big, beautiful green eyes with a shared sense of fear they both could feel but not enunciate. He longed for the flirtatious glances exchanged earlier at dinner, but now glared through eyes incapable of blinking. Soon, their instincts took over as each one's focus directed at the other with distinct admiration, and for just a few moments, all thoughts were completely consumed with the sheer joy and amazement of seeing each other completely naked for the very first time. The jeweled pendant dangled between them. Morty's body then slowly rose up from the platform. As their flesh neared, her legs parted slightly. Without provocation, Morty's engorged organ of procreation gently slid inside of her. After just a few moments, Morty heard Sarah's voice in his mind. Although they were unable to speak, he could clearly hear Sarah's voice as she chanted.

Oh my God; oh my God; oh my God; oh my God!

Sarah, he interrupted, *can you hear me?* After a short pause she responded.

Morty, what's going on? Soon they discovered that they were able to directly communicate with each other telepathically. *I'm scared.*

I know, honey. This is really strange. Try to stay calm.

Are we hallucinating?

I certainly hope so, he answered. The aliens continued to study the pair, making many gestures with their long, spindly

43

fingers as they stood quietly around the platform. Without making any effort to communicate with the young couple, they just continued to watch, void of any sound.

I swear to God, if these little bastards rape me, I'm going to be so pissed off at you, Sarah thought. *We could have done this months ago, at the beach, with a sky full of stars, and the sounds and smells of the ocean.*

Just as she finished her thought, the lights emanating from within the platform dimmed. Above them, small star-like lights appeared on the ceiling, and the distinct sound made by waves breaking gently against the seashore could be heard. The unmistakable smell of salty air from sea spray filled their noses, and a light breeze could be felt atop the skin's surface, raising small goose pimples.

I want to hear the sounds of the boardwalk, she added. With that, a faint rumbling of a rollercoaster, complete with screaming riders could be heard from off in the distance, along with carnival music typically associated with a carousel.

Sarah relaxed, and for the first time since their abduction found a moment of comfort. She was now determined to make the most of this situation, even if it turned out to be merely an illusion, or a delusion. At this point, it no longer mattered. A distinct stimulation commenced in their most sensitive regions. Neither was capable of intentionally touching the other, and no other source of the stimulus anywhere near to the couple could generate such feelings. Morty's reaction was obvious, but nestled inside of her, as it reached straight up to those virtual stars that filled the imaginary sky. Sarah's physical signs of stimulation were a little less conspicuous.

Morty, what's happening to us? As the feelings intensified, the skin of her face, neck, and chest began to redden and flush. Her breathing became noticeably heavier.

Oh my God; oh my God; oh my God. That same chant continued until they both reached climax, almost simultaneously, for their very first time, during the act of intercourse. Virtual fireworks then exploded into the quasi-sky above. As the intensity slowly waned, Sarah began to cry silently. There were tears of joy that streamed from her eyes and fell gently down upon Morty. All her contained energy was released in just one magical moment, and she now reveled in the afterglow of euphoria. Morty was also feeling quite content, as one would imagine.

I love you, I love you, I love you, she chanted, without making a sound.

I love you, too, thought Morty. They remained conjoined at their pelvic regions, completely relaxed and satisfied, before both drifted off to sleep. When they awoke, they found themselves back in Morty's car, with the radio still playing at a lowered volume. There was no longer any sign of the bright light or extraterrestrial craft that was seen earlier in the sky. Now fully dressed, there was no indication that anything unusual had taken place at all.

"What happened to us?" asked Sarah, as she righted herself in the car seat.

"I don't know," replied Morty. "What do you remember?" She thought for a moment then smiled.

"I remember the bright light, the spaceship, and the little people watching us make sweet, beautiful love for the first time." They each smiled with that thought before stopping to indulge in a soft, delicate kiss.

"Yea, that's what I remember, too," he answered. Just then, a bright light appeared through the windshield of the car. This time, it was the headlights of an oncoming automobile. Morty engaged the starter and placed his car into gear. Slowly, they drove back down the dirt path, past a car occupied by another young couple just before returning to the paved road.

Although they said very little during the drive home, both enjoyed a continued level of shared intimacy, and held each other's hand for the entire ride home. Morty checked his watch and was relieved to see that all of the night's festivities played out in just ninety minutes. During the drive, a voice from the radio stated that it was actually 11:30 p.m.

"Did you hear that?" asked Morty. "He said it was eleven thirty. My watch shows eight thirty. What's going on here?" As they passed through town, the digital clock on the side of the bank confirmed the true time. They had lost three hours during their ordeal. Sarah seemed content, without any outward sign of worry or care. Morty drove her home and walked her to the front door.

"What a night," said Sarah. "I still don't know if what happened was real or just a dream." She kissed him goodnight.

"Well, whatever it was, it was beautiful!" he answered, "and it sure beat going to the movies." After another kiss, she went into the house before Morty drove home. Once there, he retreated to his room for a much needed rest. As he lay in bed, the events of the evening kept replaying in his mind.

And with that, he heard Sarah's voice again say, *I love you.*

I love you, too, sweetheart, he thought, *now get some sleep. I'll see you soon.*

5

Wishing Aloud

Rumors of the strange fish inhabiting the creek began to spread throughout the state. Interest in the story increased to the point that it had become a favorite feature for the on-air coverage of news carriers from nearly every city. The presence of satellite vans stationed around the creek returned, as they had done just a few months earlier, only this time, there were no reports of dead bodies. Channel 4, a Capa City television station whose tag line was, "It's all news to us," lead into the featured telecast with a video production that displayed some of the contaminated fish as it cooked in a skillet.

"This aint your normal catfish. I don't care how long you cook it, it keeps squirmin'," stated Eli Benoit. He tilted a pan filled with breaded fish fillets that sizzled in cooking grease toward the camera. All elements of the meal appeared to move as if it was not only still alive, but struggling to escape from the pan. The story continued with the addition of a taped video montage depicting other native wild creatures during unusual acts of behavior. One such clip showed a bear as it struggled to walk on its hind legs, with a gait more common of one suffering from an acute case of alcohol intoxication. Another installment chronicled a group of raccoons who were also walking with an upright posture while they held out their front paws, and moved in a trance-like state. This particular conduct had been additionally captured on film as demonstrated by multiple feral cats seen along the creek's edge. No explanation was offered for these recent, and certainly bizarre events. There was, however, a correlation between all of these featured creatures who all depended on the same food sources found within the local ecosystem of the waterway for sustenance.

The next morning, Morty awoke to the sound of Sarah's voice calling in his head.

Morty, where are you? I need you here right now. His eyes opened wide, and he starred up at the ceiling. There was a short delay to his response before an appreciation of the situation.

What's the matter? He thought.

Something very strange happened to me last night. Those little freaks snuck into my room and assaulted me. At first I thought I was dreaming, but, now I know it happened. Morty's focus sharpened to process her thoughts directly as she continued. *It felt like, they got up inside of me. I don't know how else to explain it.*

Did they rape you?

No, it wasn't like that at all. It kind of felt like an examination; like the kind that is given by a gynecologist. It felt just like the exam I had at the women's center. He could feel her anxiety, so much as to raise his regard based on the intensity of her concern.

I'll get dressed now, and come over to your house this morning. Don't leave for work before I get there. He quickly dressed and brushed his teeth. Later he would return home to prepare for his first day of work at the winery, but for now, his attention was solely focused on Sarah's welfare.

In the kitchen, Ethyl began her morning by brewing a fresh pot of coffee. The inviting aroma greeted Morty as he entered the room and joined his mother. She removed a cup for him from the cabinet and prepared a hot beverage.

"Morty, do me a favor, go outside and fetch me the paper. I want to see if there are any good sales at the stores today."

He walked out the front door, then returned promptly with the newspaper and handed it to her. Bart had entered the kitchen during this time and poured himself a cup of coffee. Ethyl slid the rubber band off of the paper log and unfolded it to

48

scan the front page prior to opening the classified section. The sound of Sarah's voice returned to Morty's thoughts.

Where are you? I need to see you before I leave for work. Hurry and get over here. Morty! Bart's voice interrupted their non-verbal communiqué.

"Before you go anywhere today, I will need you to come by my office and help me bring some file boxes back to the house for storage. If you help me, and we use two cars, this can be done in just one trip." Suddenly, Sarah's voice interrupted Morty's thoughts.

Come on, Morty! Get your butt over here right now!

"Alright, already! I can't listen to both of you at the same time!" Morty blurted out loud. Bart and Ethyl both starred at their son with an air of confusion.

"Listen to both of whom?" Bart asked. Morty hesitated to reflect on his conundrum before speaking.

"Uh, sorry, Dad. What I mean is that I need to go by Sarah's house and tell her dad about my new job. I can continue to do the yard, but I'll need to find a better time to do it, probably in the morning, or during the week."

"What new job?" Bart asked.

Ethyl joined in on the conversation. "Didn't Morty tell you Papa? Our son now has a weekend job at the winery."

"Doing what?" Bart inquired.

"You're looking at the newest security guard at the Adelmani Winery!" Ethyl exclaimed, and applauded lightly with joy of the announcement.

"Congratulations, Son! That sounds like a great part-time job for you. When do you start?"

"Today, at three o'clock this afternoon. I'll be working the second shift on the weekends, and hopefully, I can pick up some holiday shifts, as well." Morty prepared himself a cup of coffee to take along for the ride. He then moved toward the direction of the front door to exit the house. "Sarah has to leave for work in a couple of hours, and I promised her I would go by their house to see her this morning, you know, to wish her good luck on her new job ."

"Don't be too long," Bart commanded. "I want to get those boxes into storage this morning. I have other things to do today."

"No problem, Dad. I'll meet you there in, let's say, about an hour."

"Send my best to the Finks," said Ethyl, before she then gave her son a proud hug with a kiss on the cheek. Bart patted him on the back as he made his way through the kitchen. Morty departed his house and drove over to Sarah's. During the ride, his mind was distracted with her earlier message until he arrived. Waiting for him on the front porch, she ran directly to his car as he pulled along the curb and parked. She forced herself into his arms as he exited the vehicle.

"I thought you'd never get here. Couldn't you hear me?"

"Yes, I could. Just calm down. You know, it's hard for me to have a conversation with someone else when you're constantly inside my head." Morty held her tight and worked to soothe her display of nervous energy. "People might begin to think we're crazy. I'm not so sure that we're not."

"I don't care what people think," Sarah replied. "I hope our little gift stays with us forever." Lucille appeared at the front door and called out to the young couple.

"Good morning, Morty. Would you like to join us for some breakfast?" Sarah pulled at his arm, physically forcing his entry into the house. Once they were inside, Lucille gave him a motherly hug and directed the pair to take their seats at the dining room table. A decorative ceramic bowl filled with pan-fried potatoes, along with serving plates of bacon, scrambled eggs, and buttered toast filled the room with a most delicious smell and sight. Morty took a seat next to Sarah while Lucille poured fresh orange juice from a large pitcher into drinking glasses. "You two eat up. Who knows when you'll get another chance for food today? I'm sure you kids will both have a busy day ahead."

"Thanks, Mrs. Fink. Is Mr. Fink home this morning?"

"No, dear. He's at the hardware store, but he should return home soon. He tends to lose track of time when he's surrounded by tools and such."

Morty continued, "I just want to let him know that Sarah and I will need to tend to the yards some time during the week. I have a new weekend job at the winery." He began to spoon food on his plate as Sarah watched him with an unmistakable look of pride.

"What type of work will you be doing?" Lucille asked.

"Morty's going to keep everyone safe. He's the newest security guard for the company." Sarah could no longer contain her joy and lunged at him with a congratulatory hug that shook the utensil out of his hand and sent it clanking onto the plate. "He has to work the evening shift, on the weekends." Lucille paused for a moment to process the information, and then smiled.

"I'm sure you two kids will still find time to see each other. Try not to let all this work interfere with your studies."

"We won't, Mom." Sarah replied with a smile. She dished out a plate of food for herself and began to eat.

"Hurry now, Sarah: You don't want to be late for your first day at work." Once they finished eating, Morty thanked the ladies for such a delicious meal. "Send our best out to your parents, Morty." Lucille added while Morty stood from his chair and excused himself from the table.

"Oh, I definitely will, and they send their best to you, as well." Sarah walked with him to the front door, but before he could leave, she snuck a playful kiss to him, far from her mother's view. He gently rubbed her tummy with the palm of his hand.

"Are you OK?" She watched his hand before looking into his eyes.

"I think so. It's still a little sore." She lightly placed her hand on top of his while he soothed her abdomen.

"Are you sure it wasn't just a dream?" Sarah looked at him with noticeable displeasure.

"Is any of this just a dream? I'm not quite sure what happened to us last night, but I'm sure glad it happened." Her eyes sank down to their joined hands. "I'll be at work until four o'clock today, and I'll be thinking about you the whole time."

"I'll be thinking about you, too." Morty replied. "Try not to get in my head while I'm driving. I don't want to have an accident." Sarah smiled and pulled at him for one more kiss.

"I can't make any guarantees, but I'll try." They continued to watch each other as he walked backward out to his car, and waved before he entered the vehicle. He continued to watch her through the mirror as he slowly drove away from the house.

Bart arrived at the office and unlocked the front door prior to Morty's arrival. The light from the back room illuminated the hallway through the suite, and that is where Morty found his father. Bart was conducting a final inventory of the contents in the storage boxes. He stopped only long enough to acknowledge his son's arrival.

"It's about time you got here. What did you do, stop for something to eat?"

"Not exactly," answered Morty. "Mrs. Fink insisted that I stay for breakfast. I didn't want to insult her by refusing." Morty directed his attention to the stack of cartons that lined an entire wall of the room. "Do you want me to start loading these into the car?" Bart stopped reading from a piece of paper that had been removed from one of the boxes and glared at his son from above the reading glasses perched on the end of his nose.

"Yea, Captain Obvious, at least I think that's what we're here to do." A smirk crossed his lips while he shook his head. "There are two types of people in this world, Son, smart asses and dumb asses; choose wisely." He pointed at the stack of boxes and then waved his hand toward to door. Morty grabbed the first box on the top and began to walk toward the exit.

The cargo was loaded into the trunk spaces of the two cars, and the men bid each other farewell before they drove away. Once back at home, the cars were parked in the driveway with the rear bumpers close to the garage door, to ease in the removal and stowage of files. Earlier that morning, Bart had cleared a specific area of the garage for stacking. The boxes were deliberately placed in a chronological order along the wall. When they finished, Barth thanked him for the help with a friendly pat on the back. Morty went into the house to clean up and dress appropriately for his first day at his new job.

He bathed and groomed before donning the required uniform provided by the winery. A moment was taken to appreciate the formal looking attire, which seemed so much more dignified than any other uniform worn for employment prior to now. Much pride was displayed as each article was added, prompting him to stand with intentional formality while checking himself in the mirror. Dark slacks, a blue, short sleeved shirt, and boots were accessorized with a black utility belt that extended an air of authority. In the kitchen, Ethyl was busy preparing a meal for Morty to take to work, and eat during his mid-shift break. She stopped to admire him.

"Let me get a good look at you, Officer Thorton!" Ethyl stated, as he entered the room. "I can't believe my eyes. You look so grown up." She straightened his collar and the laminated identification badge clipped to his breast pocket. "You be careful out there, sweetheart. I need you to come home in one piece."

"Don't worry, Mom. I'll be fine. I'm just there to keep a watchful eye on the place." He removed an apple from a bowl of fruit on the countertop and polished it against the front of his shirt. She placed the prepared food items in a brown paper bag and rolled the top closed.

"Do you have a refrigerator at work to keep your lunch fresh?" She asked while handing the bag to Morty.

"Yea. We have a small one in the guard shack." With a kiss to his cheek for luck, Ethyl patted him on the shoulder.

"Make sure you say goodbye to your father before you leave." Morty found Bart napping in his favorite reclining chair, directly in front of the television set in the family room. He approached quietly to bid his father farewell for the day.

The weekly televised golf tournament broadcast was interrupted by a developing story regarding the strange happenings to the fish and other wildlife found in and around the creek. State fish and game officials, in conjunction with the county's animal control departments, were collecting samples from any tainted remains of partial or full carcasses discovered in the region. Henry DuTray, the local representative in charge of the regional fish and game department, took part in a taped interview for the segment. Morty then noticed the copy of the daily newspaper that lay on top of the ottoman, and raised it to read the article. A large photograph on the front page depicted the same officials as the televised newscast, while they collected evidence from along the creek.

Memories of their alien abduction, together with the unexplained changes in regards to Morty and Sarah's ability to communicate telepathically consumed his attention. Bart awoke from his rest, to look up and take notice of his son, who stood before him.

"What the hell are you dressed up for, a costume party?" Morty laid the paper back down to focus his full attention at his father.

"I wish," replied Morty. "They told me it's to get the respect and attention of the employees." With a smile, he turned to leave.

"Good luck, Son," added Bart. "Don't let anyone steal all that wine."

"Not on my watch," returned Morty. He then walked through the kitchen and toward the front door. Ethyl stopped him before he could pass and gave him a supportive hug. She then handed him the sack of food as he made his way out of the house. His thoughts returned to Sarah's uninvited visitors during the night as he drove in the car. She must have felt his presence as she relayed a thought to wish him good luck on this first day at his new job.

6

Ten-Hut

The sun burned bright and high in the afternoon sky above Morty as he drove to work. Although it was a Saturday, the winery was still abuzz with considerable activity. The second shift employees entered the parking areas, while the morning shift personnel ended their work day by maneuvering their cars through the lot in an effort to leave the campus. As he approached the main gate, Morty spotted a fellow directing traffic at the entrance, who wore nearly his exact same uniform.

Encased within a light haze of rising dust, a husky man's form could be seen standing in the center of the roadway. Upon closer review, he looked to be somewhere in his middle thirties. It was then that Morty noticed the white gloves, yellow hard hat, and orange safety vest worn during traffic control. This fellow blew near constantly on a small whistle, while his hands simultaneously demanded total authority over the rush of the vehicles that entered and departed the property.

Morty slowed the car before stopping for a moment in the middle of the intersection. He wanted to introduce himself to his new colleague prior to parking the car. A shrieking noise erupted from the whistle in Morty's direction, and then the guard sternly motioned for him to keep moving through the area. As the car began to slowly move, the guard noticed Morty's attire and ordered him to stop. He marched straight to the driver's window and stuck his face inside, close to Morty's face. Behind a gleaming set of gold-rimmed aviator's sunglasses, the guard leaned through the open window with an unmistakable air of authority. Under the yellow, plastic safety cap was a close cropped hair cut, so close that beads of sweat could be seen atop the surface of the scalp. Morty reached his hand up toward the window in a gesture of greeting, only to be snubbed.

"Good morning. I'm Morton Thorton, reporting for my first day of work. I'm glad to meet you." The guard pointed at the small office adjacent to the chain link gate at the main entrance.

"You need to park your vehicle proximal to the eastern wall of the security building pronto, and remain with your vehicle until further notice!" Without any stand on ceremony for protocol toward a colleague or common decency, the guard moved away from the car and immediately returned to the task of directing traffic. Morty maneuvered his car through the crowded gate as directed, and parked near an older, well-worn, multicolored pickup truck before he shut off the engine.

This particular truck was in a rough shape, covered by contrasting, multi-colored primer-type paint that did little to conceal the collection of dents and deep scratches to the steel body panels. A modified chassis suspension raised the body of the vehicle considerably higher than most other trucks, much like those seen in an extreme off-road racing configuration. There was a safety roll bar constructed of welded three-inch steel pipe located behind the cab, complete with a row of high-energy food lamps attached along the top. Both the front and rear bumpers were made of a heavy galvanized steel, and more closely resembled the rails usually seen lining a curve on a mountain highway. Large pneumatic tires covered by a radical tread pattern like those more suited for cross-country desert racing finished the look. Scant areas of faded paint gave little cover to the steel shell, and exhibited a faded camouflage motif. The inside of the rear window was accessorized with a black metal gun rack, although no weapon was present.

Morty sat and watched as numerous employees filed in and out through the gate. He took notice as to how the female employees seemed to travel mostly in groups of four or more, wearing their white aprons and plastic safety helmets. The banter was endless, only interrupted by occasional episodes of laughter, all while remaining conscious of ongoing traffic movements. Most all of these ladies kept their hair secured in fine netting, and all wore large rubber boots to keep their feet dry from the water-soaked processing lines. By contrast, the male employees tended to enter mostly alone or in pairs, as some seized any opportunity to engage the women in conversation, invited or otherwise. Morty was startled when his attention was hijacked by the on-duty guard, who abruptly appeared at the door of his car.

"Why are you still sitting in there? Extricate yourself immediately from the vehicle and present for duty, pronto!" With a quick tug at the door handle, Morty stood from the seat, exited the car, and marched over to the office. Once inside, he scanned around the room to take a mental inventory the layout of the furniture.

A steel desk with multiple drawers and a chair were placed near the back wall in such a way that one could observe the gate through the door while sitting down. Two large picture windows on opposing walls allowed for a wide span of surveillance of the main parking lot, as well as the entrance to the property. A small refrigerator was located at the far corner, near the wall farthest from the door, along with a tall, four-drawer file cabinet. Under a protective glass frame was a large aerial map of the entire campus that hung on the far wall. Atop the desk sat a two-way radio device saddled within a battery charging unit, along with a multiple-line rotary telephone, and a ledger book for record keeping.

The guard entered the office and removed the safety cap from his head, then placed it on the desk. "My name is Suckler, Richard Suckler, but everyone calls me Sarge." Morty felt this could be his chance to break the ice and extended his hand again in greeting.

"My name is Morton, but everyone calls me Morty." There was an awkward pause. Sarge made no effort to return the gesture to shake his hand. Instead, he resumed talking with the same pitch and tone used earlier while directing traffic.

"You must report for duty at least fifteen minutes before the scheduled commencement of your shift. You must present for duty in the official uniform provided and designated for this assignment. You are not scheduled for any breaks during the entirety of your shift. If you find it necessary to relieve yourself for personal bodily functions, remember you are still on duty. You are not allowed to receive personal telephone calls or visitors while on duty." A short pause was taken for a breath.

While standing in the doorway, Morty noticed a yellow hard hat with the name, 'THORTON', handwritten on a piece of adhesive tape and affixed to the back of the gear. "Any time you leave the sanctuary of this office you must wear this helmet and this vest. Here on the desk you will notice there is a telephone. Below the protective glass cover on the desk you will find a directory containing all of the numbers pertaining to the individual departments within this facility. There are four individual lines associated with this telephone. Be sure to lift the receiver prior to pushing the blinking button on the phone. If the receiver is not lifted prior to pushing the blinking button you will terminate the call." He lifted the ledger book from the desk and opened the cover. "Before the end of each shift you are to file a report in this book. It is imperative that you only enter information that is precise and of the highest detail. If there is a disturbance, or an unanticipated event, you are required to document all names, employee numbers, license plate numbers, time of day, and any other pertinent information with regards to the incident and all witnesses or suspected perpetrators."

Sarge then sat down in the chair at the desk and opened the large book to begin writing an entry into the ledger. This specific notation documented the level of traffic and the ensuing congestion during the change of shift, and most of the communications between company leadership and himself during the first shift. Once finished, he handed the book to Morty for review. As he studied it closely, the phone rang. It was answered promptly by Sarge after only one audible ring.

"Adelmani Winery Security Department, Officer Suckler reporting. What is your concern?" He gave short, confirming replies of either "affirmative" or "negative" during the conversation, while Morty waited patiently, and continued to study the entries within the ledger. Sarge ended the call and returned the handset back to the telephone base. "I'm going to the truck repair shop on the eastern border of the property. I'll be deploying the all-terrain security vehicle for this mission. You need to remain here and monitor the main gate until further orders."

"Aye, aye, sir!" Morty replied, as he offered a half-hearted salute. Sarge then departed from the office and mounted the small, three-wheeled motorcycle parked adjacent to the building. With a quick pull of the starter cord, the cycle sputtered to life, and Sarge rode away.

Morty stood alone in the doorway of the office and spent a moment to scan around the winery grounds. Most all of the vehicle and pedestrian traffic had subsided through the parking lot and at the entry gate. Curiously, he began to inspect the items contained within the room, and the location to which each was placed. A quick glance through the window showed a person moving briskly across the paved road and toward the office. Morty paid special attention as she approached. Short and rather rotund, she moved with a labored but hastened pace. No other employees were present, so Morty wrote it off as merely a worker in jeopardy of being tardy for her daily assignment.

She was not young, and nowhere near the peak of physical fitness. Her struggle with an attempt at jogging was obvious. Morty moved to the open doorway to make visual contact and could not help but smile with the display. When she approached closer to the office, she stopped suddenly. An expression of alarm came over her face, with both of her hands placed around her neck and bent slightly forward at the waist. Tension rose as the gravity of the situation became acutely apparent. The elder woman then used her right hand and to swat at the air in his direction. Morty recognized she was using the international sign for a chocking victim. Instinctively, he exited the office and moved quickly to approach her, and then placed his hand to her shoulder to get her attention. "Are you alright?"

She removed her hands from her neck to swat at him again. A bright red hue bloomed across her face, as her eyes seemed to close and tear just a bit. It was obvious that she was unable to speak or breathe.

Morty moved into a position directly behind her to wrap both of his arms around her body and reach for the front of her abdomen. He clenched a fist with his right hand, which he then grasped with his left, and pressed deeply to the anterior area just below her breast bone. Using multiple, strong, upward compressions, the force of the action was so that he actually raised her well-nourished frame up and off the ground. This exercise was repeated until a small, round, candy that had been lodged in her throat shot completely out of her mouth; a most popular confection of peppermint flavored, hardened sugar. The expelled obstruction skipped a short distance away along the asphalt surface of the parking lot before coming to rest.

Gasps of air immediately erupted from her lungs as she began to move her right hand quickly from her forehead, to the center of her chest, and then to each shoulder, before she finally clasped her hands together and mumbled in prayer to Santa Maria. He released his grip and slowly lowered her down to a sitting position on the ground. A small tear ran down her cheek when she patted Morty on the shoulder with much appreciation.

"Gracias, señor, me salvaste la vida." She managed a smile, as she coughed repeatedly to clear the mucus from her throat. Morty smiled at her while massaging a shoulder for comfort. His Spanish was weak at best, and nearly completely ineffective for conversation.

"¿Es necesita attención de médica?" Morty asked.

"No, no, no, gracias." Morty then helped her to her feet. She rewarded him with a strong hug. As she released her hold, she gave a squeeze to his bicep and smiled. "Usted es demasiado flaca. Te traeré la comida de mañana." Morty wasn't quite sure what she just said to him, but she seemed very happy to say it. Then, under the rapid strides of a labored jog, she was gone with no more than a fleeting wave of her hand. Soon her form faded through the door of the employee entrance and she was gone.

The small piece of candy that was expelled from the windpipe of the lady rested in the parking lot. Morty thought it strange that something so innocuous could cause so much concern just a few moments earlier. It now sat motionless, about twenty feet from where Morty stood. With more than just mild curiosity for the confection, a short walk to examine the sweet tasting, red and white colored projectile ensued.

Sarge returned from the truck shop riding the off-road vehicle and parked near the door of the security office. Morty immediately abandoned any concern for the troublesome treat and returned to the building, making sure to deny Sarge any opportunity for further complaint. Morty reflected on his feat of heroism, and allowed himself a moment of reflection to his accomplishment. Such a transcendent act would translate into an earned confidence to his strut.

Sarge lifted the ledger from the desk and opened it to pen an entry to the next available page. Morty chose not tell Sarge of the events that had just happened with the lady and the candy. No identification was obtained from the woman, and therefore, no precise information to report. Sarge began to document the details of his earlier trip to the truck shop.

Benny arrived at the main gate driving a company utility truck. With a loud revving of the engine, he commanded the attention of anyone present prior to shutting it off completely. Parked obstructively at the main entry gate, traffic was effectively halted at the facility. Morty recognized his friend and met with him outside of the office and extend a proper greeting near the cab of the truck.

"Hey, Benny! How's your day going, my amigo?" Morty asked.

"Good. I was just stopping by to check on you. How's everything going on your first day with the Sarge?" Morty hesitated for a moment with a glance into the security office.

"OK, I guess," replied Morty. "He seems a little intense for this type of work. Are you sure he's not a threat to the general public?" Benny enjoyed a hearty laugh from the question.

"No, he's mostly harmless, but if you get on his bad side, you'll hear about it. I hear he keeps a nightstick stashed inside the urban assault vehicle." Benny pointed to Sarge's truck. "I wouldn't doubt if he fantasizes about using it on me. How's your first day on the job?"

"Dude, it's been crazy! I saved a lady from choking on a piece of candy. I did some quick abdominal thrusts, because she had that look to her, you know…" Morty demonstrated the technique he used to perform the maneuver on an invisible recipient.

"You saved a lady from choking?" returned Benny.

"Yup," replied Morty. "She launched a piece of candy half-way across the parking lot." He pointed to the area where treat came to rest on the asphalt. Sarge had now taken notice of the truck that Benny had parked in the roadway, and stopped writing in the ledger book. With a determined energy, he grabbed his hard hat and marched out of the office toward the truck. At the front bumper, he addressed Benny in a most authoritarian tone.

"This vehicle is illegally parked and must be moved immediately!" First, he pointed with two fingers at the truck, then to the area outside of the gate. Benny leaned his head out of the open window to the door and called out to Sarge.

"Hey, Dick! How's it hangin'?" Morty hid a smile behind his hand, but Benny did nothing to mask his amusement. Sarge did not appreciate any jocularity with the remark.

"My name is Richard!" Sarge then realized to whom he was talking. "Excuse me, Mr. Adelmani, I did not recognize you. I must respectfully request that you move this vehicle immediately. You are creating a potentially hazardous situation, as you are blocking an evacuation and emergency vehicle route.

"Don't sweat it, Dick. I need to get back to work, anyway. Good luck today, Morty. I'll check back with you later, before the end of your shift." Benny started the engine of the truck and engaged the transmission. Morty stepped back from the vehicle and waved, as Benny drove away. Sarge returned to the office and waited for Morty's return.

"I was not aware of your familiarity with the family of the company's ownership. I hope this does not present a conflict for your training." Morty quickly dismissed any concerns.

"Don't worry, Sarge. Just train me the way you think I need to be trained. I'm here to do the best job I can, and I believe you are the right person to prepare me for this opportunity." Sarge managed a slight grin before he returned his attention to writing in the ledger at the desk.

"Alright then, let's get started." Together they reviewed the most recent entry regarding the earlier trip to the truck shop. The young trainee took notice of the details in prior entries that identified personnel, vehicles, time of day, and any other pertinent information. The afternoon orientation proved to be highly informative and thorough. Things seemed to be off to a good start, as Morty began to find joy his first day, and looked forward to continued work at the winery. He liked it much more than the prior jobs that he had held of cooking chicken or cutting lawns. As the evening progressed, the air turned cool while the sun faded on the horizon. Stars began to twinkle in the darkening sky. The full moon rose to illuminate the campus with a soft, but noticeable level to allow better observation of the assets while performing observational rounding of the facility. He became more familiar with the property, and more comfortable with the expectations regarding his responsibilities. By the end of the night, Morty enjoyed a level of comfort.

Sarge's shift ended at ten o'clock, and he managed a weak salute to Morty before departing. For just an hour, Morty handled the business of security at the winery on his own, and gained a feeling of confidence in his ability to succeed at this endeavor. Relief came at eleven o'clock in the form of Carter Jamison, a low key, tall, very thin and quiet man clad in the same basic uniform required for the position. With a casual introduction and handshake, a noticeable lack of any ceremony was apparent to Carter's approach to the job. Morty recorded all the mostly unremarkable events during his shift in the ledger prior to ending the workday. Back at his car, he indulged for a moment to sit silently before leaving the winery for the evening. Sarah's voice soon filled his thoughts and took command of his mind's ear.

Morty, can you hear me? He sighed, and then thought to her.

Sarah, I hear you. It's been a long day. I'm going home to get some rest. After a short pause, the sound of her voice again returned to his thoughts.

Morty, I think you need to get over here right now. Those little bulb-headed freaks are back!

7

Caught in the Act

Morty drove straight over to Sarah's house and parked in the driveway. The porch light illuminated the entryway to the house where the front door was found to be unlocked, allowing for an easy entry. Once inside, he noticed a distinct faint glow coming from the end of the hall. It originated in Sarah's bedroom, so he cautiously made his way there. The glow became much brighter as he slowly pushed the door open and entered.

Sarah sat on the edge of the mattress, rigid but not terrified. Two humanoid beings stood silently at the foot of the bed. Their attention turned to acknowledge Morty's arrival with a slow nod of their oversized heads. Each alien stood about four feet tall, thin builds, and remarkably exaggerated extremities. Those large black eyes dominated bulbous heads, with small openings in areas where typically nostrils and ears would be located. Their mouths were undersized as well, shaped more like the soft beak of a bird. With skin of a whitish-grayish color, there were no tufts of hair, noticeable blemishes, moles, or scars. Morty moved close to Sarah and offered comfort by holding her hand.

What do they want? Morty thought to Sarah.

I don't know. They wanted you to be here, she returned. They were soon interrupted by one of the unintended visitors.

We mean you no harm. We are the same beings who studied the two of you near the creek. Sarah's grip became a little tighter. *Our craft is unable to return us to our home. We are in need of fuel.* Morty hesitated before responding.

There is plenty of fuel on this planet. We have oil, gasoline, or even nuclear fuel in power plants. What brings you here, to us? The extraterrestrial slowly raised a long, jointed, finger and then responded.

Your fossil fuels are useless to us. We require a more organic fuel source. Such fuel must be harvested while still alive and functioning. Deceased or decaying organic matter will not suffice. Our power is derived from what you would call the energy of life, the spirit, or the soul. Sarah pulled hard at Morty's arm.

What the heck do they mean? He patted her hand to comfort her nerves.

We have continued to study the two of you since our initial encounter. We trust that you will work with us, and help to complete our mission, which will allow us to return to our home. The solution instantly became obvious to Morty. The contaminated fish in the creek would make a wonderfully abundant energy source for their spacecraft, and remove a biological hazard from the community.

I need to teach you guys how to fish, and soon. Just as he completed the thought, there was a commotion at the front door of the house. Sarah's parents had returned from their evening out, and entered through the front door without much warning. With no time to escape from the room, Morty instructed the alien visitors to hide inside the clothes closet as he moved quickly to create a diversion.

"Quick, Sarah, take off your top and get under the bed covers." Confused and scared, she was slow to respond, so he instantly pulled at her clothing to remove her blouse from over her head with one forceful tug. Instinctively, she covered her chest by holding her arms crossed, and then froze with fear. Taking her by the shoulders, he pushed her down into a supine position on the mattress and then pulled at the blanket until it nearly covered her entire body, leaving only her head exposed. Next, he removed his shirt, unfastened the belt around his waist, and partially unbuttoned the trousers he wore to achieve an apparent post-coital appearance. To finish the look, he reached over and placed both of his hands on Sarah's head to ruffle her hair, and then repeated the same action on himself.

At that very moment, a light knock on the bedroom door preceded its opening, and Lucille peered inside while quietly calling Sarah's name. With an audible gasp, she covered her mouth with her hand, and gazed upon the young couple for a moment in complete shock. After a short pause to find her voice, she cried out to her husband.

"Ted, get in here now!" Sarah's father was quick to burst through the door only stop immediately in his tracks. The two parents stood stoic in total disbelief, and could only look silently upon the pair. Sarah clutched the bedding tighter against her chest, while Morty instantly fumbled to tuck his shirt and feverishly button it closed. The initial moment of silence and surprise passed for the parents, allowing Ted the opportunity to speak with a commanding tone at the young couple.

"Morty, get in the living room right now! Sarah, get yourself dressed, young lady, and get your butt in the living room, pronto!" Morty slipped past the parents and quickly walked to the front room and sat on the sofa. Ted followed, but stood along the opposite wall away from Morty, near the mantle of the fireplace, and waited for Lucile and Sarah to enter the room and take their seats. Lucille perched herself on an armchair that faced the fireplace, while Sarah took solace by positioning herself directly next to Morty on the sofa. She clutched his arm and held him tightly with a displayed expression of fear. After a short silence, Ted found the necessary words and the strength to begin a most uncomfortable conversation.

"I can't begin to explain how disappointed we are at the two of you right now. I know you are both legally adults by age, but that does not give you the right to breach our trust, and act in a most inappropriate manner. Right now, I really don't care how old you are, young lady, but as long as you are living in our home you will respect our rules. And as for you, young man, we expected a lot more from you, Morty. We have known you for a better part of your life, and have accepted you into our home as a

68

part of this family. Until now, you have always shown yourself to be an upstanding young man, but after what we have witnessed tonight, it feels as if we don't even know you anymore." Morty looked down at his feet with an expression of shame, and tightened the grip to Sarah's hand as she clutched him for comfort in a sign of unity. Lucille began to whimper quietly and struggled to hold back her tears. Ted then paused to move near her, and then stood behind the chair to massage his wife's shoulders in an effort to give comfort.

Morty looked up in time to see the two alien visitors as they moved slowly and quietly toward the front door. In a futile effort to disguise themselves, various clothes from Sarah's closet were used to aid with their escape. The first was wearing a short-sleeved T-shirt with a picture of a flying unicorn on the front, with brightly colored, red knitted leg warmers that barely clung to its skinny thighs and calves. A souvenir cap with black ears and Sarah's name stitched to the front sat atop the bulbous head. The second selected a shirt with decorative writing in metallic glitter that read, 'Don't Let Anyone Dim Your Sparkle'. This was accessorized with capris pants and knee pads usually worn for protection while roller-skating. A knitted winter's cap did little to conceal the similarly enormous head. They surreptitiously moved past the unsuspecting parents, away from their view. Sarah let out a muted gasp as she first noticed them, but quickly composed herself, so as to avoid arousing the attention of her parents.

Morty seized the opportunity to speak, and keep Ted and Lucille's attention away from the intergalactic and fashion-challenged creatures during their attempt to depart from the house.

"I can't tell you how embarrassed and ashamed I am right now, as I am sure Sarah is, as well. We both know how important it is for us to stay focused on our studies, and we try very hard to keep our feelings in check, but we are only human. Sarah is a beautiful girl, and I have nothing but the upmost respect and admiration for her, and for the two of you. I can't stop the feelings I have for her, and I know she feels the same way about me. We love to spend time together, and to share all the changes and challenges that are coming our way. I can assure you that nothing more than harmless petting went on tonight, but I also realize that this type of act is disrespectful in your home. I apologize for what went on here, but I make no apologies for the way I feel about your daughter. I know the two of you met while in college, so on some level, you must understand what the two of us are going through now."

Morty's speech took just enough time to allow the extraterrestrial visitors the opportunity to escape from within the house, and soon they quietly closed the door as they departed. Morty was shown the courtesy from his audience to finish his speech before Lucile and Ted strongly reiterated their collective desire for the young couple to exhibit restraint, but managed to give credit to each for their efforts up to this point. At lecture's end, Ted excused Morty to leave their home for the evening, but surprisingly, Sarah was permitted to escort him to the front door.

"That was quite a speech you gave back there. If I didn't know better, I would think this isn't your first time getting caught with a girl in her room."

"Don't be silly, of course this is my first time. I just didn't want your parents to see our little space friends."

"I hardly think these little freaks are our friends," Sarah returned. "Did you really mean all those things that you said tonight?"

"Of course I did. You must know how I feel about you." He pulled her close to him, and peered back into the living room, to be sure they were not being watched. Once he felt it was safe, he kissed her passionately on the lips. The encounter was hastily abbreviated when Lucille appeared and prompted his departure. Morty bid both women good-night, and then took his leave from the house. Once outside, he looked around for the aliens in their comic disguises, but did not initially see them. It was only when he entered his car that he noticed the both of them sitting patiently in the back seat.

What the heck are you two wearing?

We decided these coverings would allow us to interact with humans and not be noticed, was the response.

Yea, you two blended right in. I almost didn't see you leaving the house.

Excellent! We shall use these coverings for all future interactions with earthlings.

I was being sarcastic, thought Morty. *You two have a lot to learn about people.* He started the car and set the transmission to drive. *Let's get going on finding you two some fuel, so we can get you home. I'll take you to meet a friend of mine. He has all the gear we'll need to catch some fish.*

Before arriving at Benny's house, Morty drove to a convenience store which remained open into the late hours of the night. Live worms packaged for the purpose of fishing bait in small Styrofoam containers were kept in a refrigerator, near the display of lures and fishing line. The aliens were instructed to remain in the car, and out of sight, so as to not arouse any attention while he purchased supplies inside the store. The bait was secured and taken to the register counter. Once the transaction was complete, Morty passed again through the automatic doors, to instigate the same electric chime that announced his arrival.

A bearded, disheveled old gentleman leaned at the waist and peered into Morty's car. He weaved slightly in his stance with apparent inebriation from ingesting the contents of the bottled fluid cleverly cloaked within the paper bag held in his hand. The aliens had moved to the front seats of the car, and stationed themselves as if they intended to operate the vehicle. One sat in the driver's seat and turned the steering wheel back and forth, while the other was in the seat next to him, busily working all the switches and knobs located on the dashboard. When the old man noticed Morty approach, he offered an unsolicited assessment.

"Them's about the ugliest kids I ever saw. You ought to put them in a burlap sack and toss 'em into the river." Morty continued past the drunkard, but managed to lend a bit of his own advice as he opened the car door.

"Don't blame them. Their dad was a derelict, and their mom was an innocent sheep. Think about that the next time you're hanging out by a farm with ill intentions. I work for the county protective services, that's why I wear this uniform. These kids are being placed in protective care." The old man straightened his posture and stepped back away from the door as Morty moved to enter the car. The two were sternly motioned to move into the back seat. The drunkard then staggered away from the car and shook his head. He then walked over to the garbage can and discarded the liquor bottle before stumbling away from the storefront to disappear into the darkness.

Morty started the car and backed from the parking stall. The trio then drove out to Benny's house. It was getting quite late and Morty knew his parents would worry for his safety. He planned to call them and say he would be remaining out a little later into the night. After all that had transpired until now, he reached his destination well after the midnight hour. It took considerable persuasion to bring Benny to answer the door, and even more to invite Morty inside of the house.

"What the hell are you doing here at this late hour?" Benny asked, as he rubbed the sleep from his eyes. Morty entered the house and walked straight over to the telephone located on a table in the living room.

"Just let me call home and let my parents know that I won't be home any time soon. You won't believe what I've been through tonight." As Morty's finger spun the numbered dial on the telephone, Benny tried to close the front door against a distinct resistance. He looked to find what was causing the obstruction when the two extraterrestrials pushed their way past him and into the house.

"Holy crap!" Benny exclaimed, as he jumped back with complete astonishment, and braced himself against the wall. Morty abruptly finished the phone call to his parents just in time to turn and see his friend, who had grabbed a wooden baseball bat and raised it toward the little visitors in a most threatening manner.

"Whoa, Benny! Put down that bat and relax, I'll explain everything!" Morty fronted Benny and forcefully removed the bat from his sturdy grip. Benny again stopped to rub at his eyes, still struggling to fully comprehend exactly what was happening. "I know this is going to sound crazy, but these little guys are with me." All four beings now stood together within Benny's living room. "We need to borrow your fishing gear."

"You want to go fishing right now? Why?"

"You remember those fish that we caught at the creek? I think they may have been contaminated by those weird, little tadpoles that were found inside the stomach. I also think that we need to rid the creek of all those zombie fish, and these guys just might be the answer to that problem." Dazed, and in a bit of shock, Benny began to poke his finger at the alien's head, against the knitted cap. The small creature then slapped at Benny's hand to make him stop.

"These two want to eat fish?" Benny asked.

"I don't know about that, but I do know the spacecraft runs on organic matter. We need to teach these two how to fish and get the fuel they need to return home." The small visitors stood before Benny and began to poke at him, to which he lightly slapped at their long, thin appendages to repel their unsolicited advances.

"Why don't you just buy some fish or meat from the market? That would save you a lot of trouble."

"That's not how it works. The material must still be alive or it doesn't work." Morty continued to talk while moving the group to exit the house. Benny quit walking only long enough to secure the front door from further intrusion. "I bought some bait on the drive out here tonight. We better get started before it gets any later." The fishing tackle was collected from the garage and placed in the rear compartment of Morty's car, along with an insulated cooler and a kerosene lantern.

73

The group soon drove out to the creek and parked along the shoulder of the road, near the abutment of the Crescent Bridge. Morty and Benny carried a majority of equipment down to the water's edge, and prepared the fishing poles with hooks and bait. Morty demonstrated for those new to fishing how to properly cast the bait into the water, a task that was greeted with much difficulty at first for the pair of virgin anglers. They appeared to argue between themselves, although no sounds were uttered, and soon they began to aggressively push each other, in what could only be compared to a juvenile scuffle.

"Alright you two, settle down," Morty barked. "Here, give me those." He snatched both rods from the struggling would-be fishermen and placed one on the ground. With the other, he set the line release on the reel and demonstrated how to send the line into the water. Once the bait was allowed ample time to settle in the current, he reeled in the slack of the line and handed the pole to the first little being. Morty repeated the exercise with the second pole and all four participants were now fishing.

It didn't take long before the first strikes were hooked. Soon after a couple of fish were landed, the aliens became quite adept in the art of fishing. Benny again took commented as to how aggressively the fish attacked the bait, much like their earlier encounter, and soon the cooler was completely full of live, thrashing fish. Morty retrieved a nylon line stringer from the tackle box and began connecting the fish through the gills and mouths until all storage resources had been fully exhausted.

He began to receive messages from Sarah in his mind. She expressed concern for him and his need for safety. Morty thanked her, but insisted that she get some sleep, as it had been a day full of excitement and surely warranted some rest. Warm thoughts filled his mind until they were interrupted by the sound of Benny's voice.

"We have nowhere else to store any more fish. I think we might have to stop for the night, if we intend to keep these things alive until we're able to get them back to the spacecraft." The two little creatures communicated between themselves, then set

74

down their fishing gear. They both stared out at the water for a brief moment.

Without warning, a large, metallic structure began to rise up out of the deeper water of creek. It emerged; a round, slightly domed shaped structure that measured about ten feet in diameter. Slowly, the craft drifted along the river's surface towards them until coming to rest at the bank. A faint light could be seen along the outermost edge, and periodically changed color from white, to blue, to red. The aliens walked onto the surface of the craft and motioned the young men to follow to bring the evening's catch with them to the ship. A spherical hatch at the top the ship then opened to allow access into the vehicle. The 'Sparkle' alien pointed at the fish, and then into the orifice.

Watch your step as you board the craft. The two human friends collected the entire load of fish and carried them to the designated area. Benny looked over at Morty with an expression of amazement.

"Did you hear that? It was like that dude was talking to me without talking to me. What's that all about?"

"These guys communicate telepathically," Morty returned. "I know, it's a little weird, but you'll get used to it."

"A little weird? That's an understatement." As the fish were dumped into the hatch, the light emitted from the periphery of the craft began to brighten to a point that the outer edge of the exterior surface was now well illuminated.

Benny stood motionless, in a transient-like state of disbelief. The events of the night must have finally sank in, as he just gazed blankly as the fish vanished into the ship's opening. Morty pulled at his friend's shirt sleeve to get his attention.

"I think these guys have a pretty good handle on this now. It's been a long day and I need to get home for some rest. Are you ready to leave?" Benny's attention returned to Morty and he responded.

"Naw, man; I think I want to hang out with these guys for a little while." He looked to the little men for a response; they nodded their heads with approval. "I'll catch up with you tomorrow."

"I hope so. If you find yourself aboard that ship you may lose a little time." Morty replied. Benny's expression gave an appearance that he may not have completely understood that last statement. "Don't worry, they're harmless." He walked to the edge of the craft and stepped back onto the wet soil of the creek. As he did, a small bullfrog jumped from out of the mud near his feet and into the water, causing Morty to flinch with surprise.

The aliens closed the lid to the hatch and proceeded to bid him farewell from the edge of the ship. Although no words were spoken, Morty received thanks and gratitude from the aliens, along with assurance for Benny's safe return. He waved his hand as the craft rose completely out of the water and silently ascended into the heavens. Multiple trips were necessary for Morty to collect all of the fishing tackle, return to the car, and drive home.

He never had the opportunity to share with Benny the complete story detailing the events of the past two days. It was fortunate that Benny witnessed first-hand the alien visitors, or he may have never believed such a far-fetched tale. Nor would he believe the circumstance of the encounter that Morty and Sarah shared aboard the spaceship. With all that had transpired, he failed to relay that bit of information to Benny, but knew there would be pride for his friend in taking the relationship with Sarah to a higher level. The details of their actual consummation aboard the vessel would surely generate a good laugh. He eventually returned home a little after three o'clock in the morning. Totally exhausted, he retired straight to his bed and collapsed.

Bart and Ethyl did not disturbed his sleep, which extended well into the late hours of the morning. Instead, their plans took them out of the house early that next day. When he finally did awaken around noon, there was no need to rush to rise from the bed. As he lay there, thoughts from Sarah began to flood into his mind.

How did it go last night? Did you get rid of those things? Are you coming over? I have to work soon. Will I see you this afternoon?

Whoa, slow down, princess. I just woke up. I don't think I can get over there that quickly, and besides, I'm not sure that your parents want to see me this soon, after last night.

Her tone softened. *There's nothing to worry about. They love you, Morty. In fact, they're having Sunday brunch with your parents right now. I'm sure by this afternoon it will all be forgotten.*

I seriously doubt that, he thought. *I'll drop by your work on my way to the winery. Do you think we could go back to using the telephone instead of this telepathy stuff? It kind of freaks me out.*

Are you crazy? I love this, and I hope it never goes away!

Alright then, you need to get out of my head for now. I have things to do. I'll see you this afternoon.

He arose from his bed and proceeded into the kitchen. There he found a plate of food that had been prepared earlier by Ethyl, and placed inside the refrigerator. After eating, he gathered his uniform that now reeked with the smell of fish, and cleaned it along with the other dirty clothes of the laundry. He then spent the remainder of the morning tending to the weekly chores in the yard. Once the task was finished, he dressed for work, and prepared a small meal to take for later. There was a need to leave a little early, as he promised Sarah a visit to her place of employment prior to reporting for his own.

8

Room for Change

Morty drove in his car out to Mercy Gulch and parked in a lot near Madame Souris' Boutique and entered the store. A faint tinkling sound emanated from a pair of small bells attached at the top of the door frame that quietly announce his arrival. A casual reception of glances from the female patrons greeted him once inside. It was quite unusual to see a young man in this establishment, and the security officer uniform he wore demanded even more scrutiny. Sarah noticed as well, and moved swiftly to address him near the entrance.

"Hello handsome," she said, before grasping the front of his shirt to pull him close enough for a kiss. She intentionally coated his lips with a bright red cosmetic in a most generous manner. "I was worried you wouldn't make it here today." Sarah looked quite professional, wearing a gray, knee-length skirt that clung tightly to her petite figure. By contrast, a billowing, sheer, red satin blouse over a black tank top with slender straps on the shoulders completed the look. Her hair was pinned up to allow everyone the opportunity to easily admire the pendant necklace recently received as a gift on her birthday.

"You look fantastic! Morty said. She acknowledged his compliment with a warm smile. "How's work going today?"

"It's been busy. A lot of ladies are shopping for the upcoming holidays. If this keeps up, I'll make more in commission than I will in wages." She took a moment to straighten the collar of his shirt and attempted to remove the lipstick smudge from around his mouth.

"Don't wipe that off," he barked. "I want to taste your kiss later, when I'm at work."

"That is so sweet," she replied, and then quickly kissed him again to replace the lost smudge with more of the makeup.

"I better get out of here before you get into trouble." Morty pulled back away from her in an effort to leave, and loosened the grip of her hands as he moved to retreat.

"Don't go yet; I'm not ready." She pulled him by the hand hastily through the store into the back of the building, near a row of fitting rooms along the far wall. "Hide in here and wait for me. I'll be back in a bit." With a sharp push, he was forced into the small changing space and the door was closed.

Multiple garments hung from the many wardrobe hooks inside the small room. Attached to one wall was a floor-length mirror, and a chair for convenience. Women's voices could be heard just outside of the room, engaged in conversations prudent to shopping for high-end apparel. Those voices grew louder as they drew closer, and prompted Morty's concern of discovery. Such worry proved warranted when the door handle was turned. Without option, the garments hanging from the hooks were removed and held suspended in a desperate effort to conceal his face and body from certain detection. Sarah was keen to the problem, and moved quickly to address the patron.

"Could I provide you with any assistance in the dressing room today, madam?" Sarah was heard to ask.

"No thank you, child," was the reply. "If you would be kind enough to help me through the door, then, I can do the rest."

The door creaked open slowly allowing Sarah the opportunity to peer inside of the small room. Through her young eyes, she could easily make out Morty's form behind the suspended garments that were held in his hands. His lower extremities were weakly disguised behind the chair. Fortunately, the considerable thickness of the bifocal lensed glasses the matron wore restricted her vision, and perhaps her awareness.

"This room is in need of attention," announced Sarah "Please let me show you to another room." The customer shrugged off the remark and continued on her way.

"This room will do just fine, child. Now you go and help those other ladies, and I will call you if I need you."

Get me out of here! Morty thought to Sarah.

I can't, was her reply. *Just stay in there until I can think of something.*

The elderly woman entered the room toting multiple garments draped against her shoulder, secured by her grasp of the hooks of the clothes hangers. Sarah could now only smile, and discretely toss Morty a wink of her eye for luck before she closed the door. With aged and frail hands, the garments were slowly hoisted until secured on what she thought were wall hooks, but were actually the ends of his outstretched fingers.

The extra load weighed heavily on his hands, but he worked to remain motionless, frozen with the fear of being discovered in a woman's dressing room. That terrifying thought repeated continuously in his mind, causing small beads of perspiration to form on his brow. The fluid burned slightly when it trickled down into the outer edges of his eyes. That same sweat now blurred his vision, but he did not dare to wipe it away. The woman then turned to stand before the mirror, and take notice of her mature figure. The kyphotic curvature of her upper spine gave a stance with a lean forward that pushed her primary line of sight directed downward at the floor. She was a well-dressed lady, with thinning hair that had been professionally set to give an appearance of a being a little bit thicker; silver in color, with just the slightest hint of a blue hue. Multiple gold bracelets and rings clanked together with her every movement, as the arthritic hands fumbled to slowly unbutton her blouse.

Morty tightly clinched his eyes closed, in an attempt to keep out the burning sensations caused by the mounting sweat on his face, and to avoid bearing witness to the events about to play out within his line of vision. Due to an unwavering need to stay abreast of the situation, he strained to keep open his eyes.

The blouse was the first garment removed and placed carefully on an empty hanger to avoid any wrinkles to the fabric. As she turned away from the mirror, Morty was introduced to the

80

largest brazier that he had ever seen in his life. There were multiple rows of clasps along the wide band of fabric along her back that supported two mammoth fabric cups that suspended her considerable breast tissue at the level of her pelvis.

Sarah! You have to help me! I'm trapped in the dressing room with somebody's grandmother! Get in here quick, she's almost naked! Morty's thoughts to Sarah were direct and desperate. He paused momentarily for her reply. Almost instantly, there was a light tapping at the door. Sarah spoke with a soft voice.

"Hello, Madam. Is there anything I can help you with in there?"

"No thank you, sweetie. I've got everything I need right here. I'll call you if I need your help." She then reached over to her hip and struggled to unzip the fastener of the skirt in a display of obvious effort. The slow-motion strip tease display continued to play out, much to Morty's chagrin, with no chance for an escape. He cringed at the sight of the wrinkled and sagging skin on the backs of her arms, and how they seemed to move as if under the influence of some phantom breeze that passed within the dressing room. With the zipper now open, she reached back with her hand for support in her stance and pressed against the garments that Morty held up in disguise. The pressure of her hand against his lower pelvis, in a most sensitive area, caused the release of a muffled yelp.

Sarah, I'm dying in here. You have to do something right now, he thought. The elderly lady slipped out of her skirt, and carefully placed it atop the back of the chair to preserve the freshly-pressed look to the fabric. There she stood, in just her barest of essentials, knee-high stockings, and patent leather shoes. Morty was now subjected to the largest pair of panties he had ever seen, and could not divert his attention.

Then, in a last act of desperation, he bowed his head and prayed to a loving and caring God to show mercy through an act that would allow an escape. He bartered with promises of saintly acts to those less fortunate, and a vow of weekly attendance at a

81

local house of worship. Finally, he telepathically reached out to the alien visitors with a request for repayment of his favor in providing a fuel source for their disabled craft.

She reached for the dress that was brought into the room and labored to remove it from the clothes hanger. After the zipper was opened, she turned back toward the mirror and held the garment against her body, then raised it above her head to slip it on and check for a proper fit.

Morty recognized this opportunity to flee, and dropped all of the items that were held within his hands. With the garment obscuring her vision, he moved past her in a flash, and grabbed at the knob to open the door. Free from the confines of the fitting room, he wasted no more time in moving directly to the main entrance of the store. With only a wave back in Sarah's direction, he was soon outside and running straight to his car.

The commotion caused quite a stir with the women shoppers, but no one seemed to be quite sure as to what they had just witnessed. Sarah moved quickly to the exit and obstructed anyone from passing through the open doorway. The idea was to keep others from venturing out into the parking lot. She held the door closed to give the appearance of protecting those within the building. Her true motive was not to let anyone get a better look at Morty, or leave the store with merchandise yet to be purchased and tallied for a sales commission.

Be careful at work tonight! I'll talk to you soon! Stay out of trouble! Those telepathic thoughts followed as he fled.

Yea, princess, I'll see you soon! Morty thought back to her as he ran. He entered the car and drove quickly to the edge of the parking lot. A big sigh of relief withdrew from his chest as the rivers sweat were wiped from his face by the back of his arm. He continued straight to the winery and did not stop until he was safely within the designated area for security employees' parking. Sarge was again busy with directing traffic at the plant entrance, his white gloves moving in perpetual motion and a near constant blaring of his whistle. Morty gathered his lunch and readied himself for work. In the office, he placed his food in the refrigerator, and then sat at the desk to allow himself a moment of rest. While there, he scanned the ledger for the most recent entries regarding the workplace.

Benny stopped in the company vehicle at the gate near the office door. It was a small diesel-powered truck that looked to be about half of the size of a typical truck more often seen hauling freight on the interstate. He jumped down from the cab and slammed the rickety door closed. The truck engine continued to idle.

"Hey, Morty!" Benny called out to his friend, as he walked to the office doorway. "I still can't believe what happened last night. I can hardly wait to see what you have planned for us tonight." Morty looked up from the pages of the ledger and managed a smile.

"I hope the most exciting thing that happens tonight is a quiet shift of guarding this property. If our little visitors do show up, I'll just send them your way."

"Hell yea! Those little guys were a blast! We didn't finish fishing until their fuel tank was full, and then we gigged for frogs, just for good measure. By the time we finished, we had filled the cooler, too. They took all that away with them and said they'd get back to you on that zombie fish problem." Benny was quite animated with his hand movements and facial expressions as he spoke. "After they dropped me off at my place, they took off, straight up, and disappeared. I didn't get to sleep until after sunrise."

Traffic at the main entrance was soon reduced to a crawl, due to the truck obstructing the flow of roadway. This fact was not lost on Sarge, who moved hastily toward the gate. All vehicular movement came to a complete stop. Sarge charged toward the truck accompanied by the ear-piercing shrill of a small metal pea whistle securely held between his lips, as he waved both hands high above the level of his head. It didn't take long to discover that there was no driver in the cab, and his next destination was the security office to investigate. Once there, Benny was instantly recognized, which gave pause to Sarge, followed by a slow sway of his head, and an expression of utter disgust.

"I should have known it would be you. Anytime there's a problem, you always seem to be standing squarely in the middle of it." Sarge then backed away from the office and walked directly to the front bumper of the idling truck. "This vehicle must be moved immediately!" Illegible words directed toward the stopped cars ensued as he soon returned to take control of the stalled traffic situation. Using precise pointing and spinning motions of his arms and hands, movement of the automobiles resumed, as did the incessant blowing of the whistle. Benny smiled to Morty and departed with a few words of encouragement while he walked out toward the truck.

"Good luck tonight, buddy. If you need anything, just call me on the radio. You've got this." He climbed into the cab and called out through the window. "If those little guys show up tonight, let me know." The transmission of the truck made a grinding sound as it was placed into gear. With a blast of the air horn, Benny drove into the cluster of assembled cars with the wave of his hand.

Sarge jumped back in surprise with the sound of the horn, and then dodged the approaching bumper of the shuttle truck and returned to the task of traffic control. Once the transition to the evening shift was complete, a notation was made by Sarge in the ledger with regards to Benny's earlier antics without regard to public safety. With his scheduled shift at an end, Sarge collected his personal effects and exited the property without extending as much as a cordial farewell. Morty would now be on his own for the remainder of the shift, but took comfort in knowing his best friend was never too far away if needed.

The flow of people and their vehicles during the change of shift filtered down to just a trickle. Morty found himself standing in the doorway of the office, watching as the last of the stragglers made their way into the numerous buildings. Emerging through the dust of the parking lot appeared the same lady for whom he provided assistance for the day before. She again walked with a hastened pace, but today, she balanced a plate of food covered with aluminum foil. The employee badge attached to her shirt collar identified her as Reña Cuajo, employee number 81570. She walked in a direct line toward Morty and handed him the dish.

"Este alimento para usted." He graciously accepted the gift with a smile.

"Esto es especial. Gracias. Thank you," he replied, and she smiled back at him. With that, she resumed her march to work after giving a friendly pat to his shoulder. He then entered the office with the offering and carefully pulled back the foil that covered the paper plate. Reña had prepared a dish consisting of three tamales still inside their corn husks, with generous helpings of refried beans and seasoned rice. It was still a little warm and smelled delicious, and without any doubt, much more enticing than the ham and cheese sandwiches that were prepared earlier at home and brought to work. The foil cover was returned to the food before the plate was placed on top of the small refrigerator to finish cooling. Morty's attention returned to his responsibilities of his work as the most recent entries to the ledger were closely reviewed. Inside were documentations of the usual hourly findings; trucks go in, and trucks go out, as well as private automobiles and employees. Rarely would there be a noted disturbance that required police or emergency medical responders; by all accounts, most days were very routine.

Morty began to view the job as a blessing and a curse. It paid well enough to compensate for the reduced number of hours worked, and afforded him ample time to study while on duty. For this he was grateful to his friend, and made every effort to show his appreciation by giving his best to do a good job. On the other hand, he yearned to spend more time with Sarah, as their feelings for each other intensified. Their newfound ability to communicate through telepathy proved to be rather amazing, and the couple indulged with every opportunity.

Benny would check in with Morty at the gate occasionally when the shuttle truck was without any load of product. Morty shared the bounty of prepared food and sandwiches at the mid-shift break. After sufficient amounts of grapes were delivered for processing to the employees, Benny ended his day of work. Having started at noon, he now felt the sting of fatigue. The late night fishing excursion and subsequent refueling activities of the evening prior caught up to him.

Benny bid farewell, but extended an invitation to stop by the house after work. Morty was quick to decline, as Sarah had called out multiple times during the shift. She made her feelings known, and longed to resume their earlier meeting which was cut short. Her tenacious use of telepathy was unrelenting. The plan was made to sneak out of the house to meet with him down the street.

Morty agreed, but under duress. To meet up this late given the recent events that had transpired with her family did not seem like the best of ideas. Her insistence proved more than could be suppressed, so from a safe distance away from the Fink's residence, the car was parked and he waited. Sarah appeared from an area of thick shrubs, familiar from a time when they were young and played games throughout the neighborhood.

"Hey you! What took you so long?" Sarah leaned in through the open window of the door and initiated a display of affection that made him smitten with appreciation. Between kisses, he began to plead his case.

"I didn't get out of there until eleven o'clock, and then I drove over here as fast as I could. How was the rest of your day at work?" The question gave pause and her expression turned more serious.

"Well, you caused quite a commotion with the ladies at the store. My manager wanted to call the police and file a report. No one could understand what a security guard was doing inside the dressing room." A coy smile then crossed her lips. "Luckily Ms. Frangible, who was the lady in the room with you, in case you didn't get her name, did not get a good look at you, so there was no reliable eye witness descriptions to file any report." Sarah leaned further into the car and closer to him. "Maybe the next time, I'll get to join you in the dressing room?"

"I seriously doubt there will be a next time, as I will never return to that store." Morty spoke with a distinct austerity to his voice. "There will be no future visits to the boutique for me. You are going to get us into too much trouble." The rush of adrenalin experienced during his flight outweighed her sense of decency. With Sarah's tug on the door, he gently pulled the release handle and exited the car. They soon embraced and she could feel his tension.

"Come on, Morty, relax. When you think about it, today was very exciting!" She pushed him back against the fender of the car and playfully tried to unbutton his shirt. "My parents think I'm asleep in my room. Take me out for a ride to the creek. Hopefully we'll get abducted again." He grabbed her hands in an effort to retain his clothing.

"OK, now, settle down." First, he held onto her hands with a firm grip, and followed that by tickling her along the abdomen until she released her hold on his clothing. "As fun as that sounds, it's been a very long and exhausting day. I need to get home for some much needed sleep. I have clinic tomorrow and you have your first day of college. Let's put today to rest and get ready for tomorrow."

She relented with a pout of her lips, then gently gave him a kiss good-night. "Will I see you tomorrow?"

"Absolutely, I'll come by your house after I finish at the clinic." They parted ways for the night, and Morty hurried on his way home. Upon arrival, there was surprise to find his parents still awake at this late hour. Seated at the dining room table, Ethyl was obviously upset, nearing tears, as Bart displayed reservation with his emotions. Both were drinking coffee, most unusual for this late hour of the night. Morty knew his parents had spent considerable time with the Finks during the day, and suspected that they must have shared the events of the prior evening regarding Morty and Sarah in her room. This would surely prove to be a difficult and sobering conversation. He took a seat with them at the table. "Is everything OK?" Ethyl wiped away her tears with a napkin, but could not compose herself enough to speak.

"Morty, we need to talk." Bart used a most somber tone with his voice. There was a distinct sense of loss or grief. "Your brother called tonight." He struggled to find the appropriate words to continue. "I don't know if he will be joining us for Thanksgiving this year. Apparently, your brother has kept a secret from us for a long time." Bart's voice began to crack, and he struggled to continue. "You're brother has informed us that he has decided to come out." There was an uncomfortable pause to the conversation.

"I'm confused. Do you mean he's coming out for Thanksgiving, or not?" Ethyl could no longer suppress her sadness and began to wail. Bart moved to console his wife. "That's a good thing, right?"

"Yea," continued Bart with a slow pace to his words. "Let me just cut to the chase; your brother has informed us tonight that he is gay." Bart's words were deliberate.

"You mean, like happy?" Morty asked. Ethyl again sobbed out loud.

"Not quite, son." Bart struggled to find the appropriate words to continue. "Sheldon, it seems, is a homosexual. He said that, he has struggled for some time with his sexuality and has decided that now is the time to share that information with the family. He also said that, if we don't welcome his partner into our home for the holidays, then he won't be here with us either."

Morty absorbed the news without much problem, but could appreciate the shock caused to his parents. He knew his brother was not one to chase the ladies, and seemed more partial to spending time with his male friends. Absent were the typical bikini-clad posters of women adorning the walls of his bedroom, or magazines that featured young ladies photographed during various stages of dress; the one's commonly found hidden beneath the mattress of most pubescent young men. Times were changing, and there was a growing acceptance with regards to such progressive personal lifestyles. For Bart and Ethyl, that progress had yet to infiltrate their generation of peers. Only time and deep reflection could help to bring a sense of peace and understanding to their troubled minds.

As it turned out, the recent news involving Sheldon caused such a stir, that his parents made no mention as to the events on Saturday night at Sarah's house. Morty thought it would be in his best interest not to raise such a subject at this time. Certainly Ted and Lucile must have discussed it at brunch; how could they not?

He reached out to his mother with a firm, consoling embrace, followed by a sympathetic pat to Bart's shoulder before taking the opportunity to retire for the night. Too exhausted to give much thought to anything but rest, he found the bed warm and welcoming. Sweet sleep, much overdue, ensued.

9

Rising Son

The unrelenting buzz from the alarm clock ushered Morty into the new day. Streams of sunlight forced their way through the near totally shuttered blinds. The energy within the house remained still, as the parents held refuge from within their bedroom; not to show their faces during the entire morning routine. A quick shower proceeded his donning of attire of a more professional nature for his day at the clinic. To keep up his strength, a light meal consisting of a bagel with a slice of cheese and a cup of coffee were quickly consumed, along with information he attained from a quick scan of the morning newspaper retrieved from the driveway and brought into the house.

The lead story on the front page ran with a bold heading that read: Strange Times Return to Grizzly Creek.

State game warden Hank DuTray was photographed as he knelt at the edge of the creek and collected samples of water and soil for detailed analysis. Talk of déjà vu began to influence public speculation, as similarities to the unusual events which occurred earlier that same year began to circulate. Those incidents resulted in three deaths, all under strange circumstances and all yet to be explained. Luckily, there had been no fatalities or serious illnesses associated with the recent contaminated wildlife, but the authorities were taking no unnecessary chances, and issued a stern warning with regards to consuming any fish or game procured from along the waterway.

Bart emerged from the bedroom wearing pajamas over a bath robe, and entered the kitchen to pour a cup of coffee for

Ethyl. Morty addressed his father by lowering the paper, and made eye contact during their conversation.

"How's Mom doing this morning?"

"She's still in bed, but she's coming around," answered Bart. "Have you finished reading that paper?"

"Yea, here you go." The paper was folded in half and then handed to his father. "I have to get to the hospital. I don't want to be late on my first day of clinic." Bart turned to proceed back to the bedroom, when he suddenly stopped to address his son.

"You know, your mother and I have never waned in our love for you boys. All this recent talk changes nothing about our love for your brother, Sheldon, or our feelings for you. Your mother has a bit of a selfish side to her that anxiously awaits the arrival of grandchildren." With a pause, Bart looked into the cup and reflected, so as to carefully choose his next words. "I don't want you to confuse your mother's disappointment with desperation." Another respite followed as he waited for confirmation of the young man's understanding to such a delicate matter. Morty smiled and nodded his head. "Be careful out there, son, and always remember that we love you." Bart reached out to give his son an awkward, single-armed hug before returning to his room.

Morty paused for a moment to mentally digest the information. This was the first time that he could recall such an unforced display of affection by his father; uncharted and foreign territory within their relationship since early on in his childhood. The moment passed, and so he quietly collected his lab coat and school supplies before departing for the hospital. During his drive to Mercy Gulch, his thoughts remained with Sheldon. How difficult it must have been for him to confide to his parents the deep, dark secret that he had kept from them for so long, and apparently from most everyone else, as well. Why would these types of feelings deserve such scrutiny? It seemed as though his parents were trying to shield both of their sons from experiencing any feelings of love. Even though he didn't really understand the reasons behind Sheldon's preferences, Morty was not naive to the meaning of homosexuality. A shiver then ran through his body. His thoughts turned to Sarah, and she soon responded.

Good morning handsome. Are you thinking of me?

Yes, I am, he thought. Well, kind of, Sheldon came out to my parents last night. My folks are taking it pretty hard. They didn't even mention anything about what happened with us, at your house, on Saturday night.

Your brother came out, from where? Her naiveté was a welcomed bit of comic relief.

That's sweet. No, girl, Sheldon is gay. He told my parents yesterday. My mom seems upset, and my dad just acted disappointed, but he always acts disappointed. Morty thought to himself for a moment. *That's the first time I can remember Sheldon disappointing my father. I have to go, now. I'm nearly at the hospital. I'll catch up with you at lunch time. Be safe and have a great day.* She wished him the same, and he returned his attention back to driving. The car was then parked in the adjoining lot before he entered the hospital.

Once inside the radiology department, he slipped on his lab coat and then checked the pockets for all the necessary supplies: lead right and left film markers, a writing pen, and a small book that outlined radiology exam positioning with technical settings for the equipment. Donna Stump, his classmate at the hospital, also prepared herself for the day. The two nearly collided into each other at the main entrance to the department. After she recovered from the initial shock, greetings were extended to him through a pleasant tone in her voice, and a smile.

"Hey, Morty. How are you today?"

"Great, Donna! How are you?" He returned the smile.

"I'm doing very well, thank you for asking. What area are you scheduled to work in today?"

"I'll be in fluoroscopy. The list of patients looks pretty full. It should be a busy day. Where are you today?" A printed patient schedule was posted on the wall. Donna moved closer in an effort to better study the registry.

"Judging by the number of mammography cases, I'll be buried in boobs all day," she said in a doleful tone. Morty could not help but smile with the idea. "Trust me, it's not the fantasy dream scenario that you obviously have going on inside of your head. These women are quite older, and I think if you saw what was actually going on in there, it might change the way you think about breasts." A feigned effort was made to mask his amusement, for which he parleyed a response.

"So, what you're saying is, the fantasy in the mystery."

"You just may be correct in your assumption, and I recommend that you leave it there." Donna let out a slow breath through a courteous smile, and then proceeded on to her ultimate destination, the mammography examination rooms. Morty made his way to the fluoroscopy room. Sally Dalton, a staff technologist, prepared for the first case of the morning. The two had met a week earlier when Morty paid a visit to the hospital to introduce himself to the staff. A paper requisition had been placed on the counter by the sink. He drew the document close, in an effort to read the details of the examination with regards to the patient's medical history. An upper gastrointestinal procedure was prescribed for a seventy-three year old man. The patient's symptoms which warranted the test were documented as esophageal reflux with associated pain after consumption of moderately seasoned foods. Sally entered to see Morty standing near the cabinet countertop and greeted him.

"Good morning, Morty. Will you be working with me today?"

"Yes ma'am," he answered. "By the looks of the schedule, we're going to be quite busy."

"After the first two U.G.I.'s, we have a barium enema to perform before our morning break. Have you ever seen a B.E examination before?"

"Not yet, but I'm looking forward to it?"

"I wish I could say the same, but after doing hundreds of such exams, I guess it's not so special to me anymore. You'll know what I mean when you've been at this for a few years." She smiled and resumed the preparation of the room for the first exam. "Would you mind finding the patient in the waiting room and bringing him back? Be sure to stop at the dressing rooms and have him change into a couple of gowns."

"No problem, I'll be right back." He exited the room with the requisition and moved briskly to the main registration area. There he found multiple patients seated as they waited for their respective scheduled exams to be performed. Some were there for mammography, while others for computerized tomography, ultrasonography, and other routine radiology exams.

Patients of all ages and backgrounds awaited care. Morty read the name from the requisition.

"Abel Anderson!" An elderly gentleman acknowledged his name with a wave of his hand and rose to his feet. Morty approached with salutations.

"Hi, Mr. Anderson. My name is Morty and I will be helping you with your exam today. Come with me and we'll get you started." He directed the patient toward the changing rooms, then handed out two hospital gowns along with a plastic garment bag. "Before we go any further, can I get your full name?"

"Abel A. Anderson," was the direct response from the patient.

With a smile, Morty asked, "What does the 'A' stand for?"

"Ah?" The old man responded comically as he leaned forward with his hand cupped to his ear. The smile was reciprocated.

"What then, is your date of birth?"

"To be honest with you, I was pretty darn young back then, so I don't remember so well." He produced a wallet from the front pocket of his trousers and fumbled as he opened it to display an identification card located inside. Morty confirmed this was indeed the correct patient for the exam. They continued on to the changing rooms. The patient was then instructed how to dress.

"I need you to step into the dressing room and remove your shirt and slacks. Please leave your underwear on for this exam. Place the first gown on with the opening to the front, and then the other with the opening along your back, so that you are completely covered." Morty demonstrated with his hands, as to where the openings should be once he was dressed.

"That's good," replied. "I don't want to walk around this place with my butt hanging out. The only draft I like comes out of a keg, not my clothes."

"Also, if Sister Bonaventure catches you wearing only one gown, it will be my butt that will be hanging out, on the street, that is." Morty had been forewarned as to the administrator's strict standards, and continued with his instructions. "Put all of your clothes and valuables into this bag, and remember to bring your belongings out of the dressing room with you. Have a seat in one of these chairs and I will be back with you in just a few minutes."

The door of the small room was politely held open to allow the older gentleman to enter with ease. Morty then closed the door and returned back to the exam room.

The X-ray table was tilted into an upright position, with the foot stand attached at one end and secured. The fluoroscopy image intensifier tower had been retracted to allow easier access to mount the platform. Multiple cups containing the barium meal sat on the counter, along with a small portion cup that held a few ounces of baking soda crystals. These crystals, when swallowed with water, would create gas within the stomach to allow expansion of the gastric folds to increase the visualized surface areas of the stomach. Spot film cassettes were made readily available for the capture of static images taken during fluoroscopic viewing utilizing the intensifying tower. The nine-by-nine inch cassettes were stacked on the counter, far away from the X-ray source to avoid premature exposure of the radiographic film contained within.

Sally returned to the room and asked Morty, "Where's our patient?"

"I sent him to change into the gowns. I'll go check on his progress." Morty went back to the small room to confirm the readiness of the older gentleman. Abel had indeed changed into the provided hospital gowns and sat patiently on a chair outside of the dressing room. Morty directed him to the prepared examination room and they entered together. Sally introduced herself before addressing the patient in regards to the procedure, and answered any questions regarding what to expect from the experience. The radiologist soon entered the room and promptly introduced himself.

"I'm Doctor Esofobea, but you can call me Doctor 'E': It's nice to meet you." The doctor moved to a position near the table and guided Abel as to where to stand atop the foot board. "What type of problem have you experienced to warrant this exam?" Abel thought for a moment then responded.

"About a week ago, I was at a friend's house for dinner. We fried up some catfish that he caught earlier that day, out at the creek. They were some pretty good eatin'. We breaded and fried 'em up in a skillet with some potato wedges, green beans, onions, and some bacon for flavor. Well, it was delicious, and I didn't notice any problems until later that night. It felt like my bowels were in motion all night, and then, I don't remember much else for about two or three days. I live with my daughter's family, and she said that I just sat around watching television. She said I was in some kind of trance, or something, like a zombie. She was afraid this might be a reaction to my medications, or a stroke, and insisted on taking me to the doctor. Come to think of it, I can't remember if we went to see him or not. I don't remember things so well lately, but it's getting better."

"Are you still having problems after eating food?" asked the doctor.

"No, not really. I think there might have been something wrong with that fish, or something."

"Perhaps. Let's get started and take a look. I need you to lean back against the table."

The fluoroscopy tower was moved and locked into position before the patient was handed the baking soda crystals and a small cup of water. After ingesting those items, the barium meal was swallowed before any radiographic images could be obtained. The esophagus was thoroughly visualized prior to the table being lowered into the horizontal position. Abel was then instructed to roll into different positions and allow the dense liquid to coat the entire inner surface of the stomach. Multiple exposures were then captured by the doctor as the column flowed deeper into the alimentary tract. Additional imaging followed by the technologist. Once all of the static films were checked for quality, the exam was completed, and the patient was thanked for his cooperation. Abel required some assistance from the table before he was escorted to the dressing room and released from care.

In the film review area, or 'light room', Morty closely studied all the images before Sally could collect the films for the patient's folder. Along with the requisition, all were submitted to the radiologist for final interpretation. The next exam of the morning was another upper gastrointestinal case that progressed in a near identical fashion as the first. The room was again reset, and Morty was instructed to prepare the equipment for an examination of the large bowel, otherwise known as a barium enema.

The examination table remained flat with the fluoroscopy tower retracted. From within the cabinet, a fifteen-hundred cubic centiliter bag was removed. Sally assembled all of the items necessary for the procedure on the counter. Contained within the sealable bag was a white barium powdered substance. A long, clear plastic tube was attached at one end. A sealed flap allowed for water to be added to the barium creating a liquid suspension, and the tube permitted a special tip to be connected, as a way to deliver the fluid to the patient. The invasive end of the instrument was fitted with an inflatable bladder that, once inserted into the rectum and expanded, made a tight seal to anchor the tube and its liquid contents tight against the anal sphincter. The bag was hung from a pole, and the plastic tube was cleared of any unnecessary air within the line. A pair of latex examination gloves and a generous amount of glycerin based lubricant on a paper towel would be needed to aid in the initial introduction of the instrument.

Walter Sunderland, an elderly gentleman well into his seventh decade of life, was then summoned from the waiting room and directed by Morty to remove all of his clothes in the changing room. Again the patient was instructed as to the proper way in which hospital gowns were to be worn. All personal belongings were secured in a plastic bag and brought into the examination room. When Walter entered, the table was in the horizontal position, and he was prompted to sit on the table.

"Good morning, Mr. Sunderland. My name is Sally, and this is Morty. Morty is a student from the college, in the radiology technologist program, and he is here to learn. I will be assisting you with your examination, and Morty will be assisting me. Have you ever done this type of procedure before?" She motioned with her hand to the bag filled with the white liquid which hung from the pole. He squinted his eyes in an attempt to better focus his vision.

"That looks like an enema bag. Is that what we're doing?" He spoke with a booming voice.

"Yes, sir. Have you ever had a cleansing enema?" He nodded his head.

"I've had problems with constipation in the past, that's why I'm here."

"OK, then let's get started. What we are going to do is place this tube into your rectum. There is a balloon at the end that will be inflated once it is inside of you. The balloon will hold the tube in place and reduce any chance of leakage. You will feel pressure in your rectum, and you may feel as if you need to have a bowel movement; this is normal, so please do not try to push it out. The doctor will then come into the room and instruct us to begin filling your colon with this white fluid. You will feel even more pressure, but do the best you can to tolerate it, and we will work as fast as possible to get you through this exam. Once we finish, we will drain the water from you and get you in the rest room. When you feel as if the water has been expelled, we will come back to this room for one more picture. Do you have any questions?"

He shook his head. "No, let's get this thing over with." The patient was instructed to roll onto his left side, with his right leg slightly bent forward. Sally instructed Morty to put on the examination gloves. Under her watchful eye, the enema tip was generously coated with lubricant and gently eased past the anal opening and into the rectum. Walter expressed mild discomfort as the instrument made contact with a large external hemorrhoid at the anal orifice. With the tube in place, the balloon was inflated slowly by squeezing a small plastic bulb multiple times, and then clamped to keep it inflated. The radiologist entered the room and introduced himself.

Morty was instructed to open the clasp on the tube to allow the barium to flow into the patient. As the colon filled, the doctor instructed the patient to turn slightly from side to side, and to hold his breath. Images confined to specific areas of the anatomy were captured using the X-ray equipment. Dr. Esofobea completed his portion of the test and the fluoroscopy tower was retracted. Sally positioned the overhead X-ray tube unit for procuring larger images of the entire bowel. Morty selected the largest cassette available, fourteen by seventeen inches, and secured it into the sliding film holder, or Bucky tray, located within the table. The tube, Bucky, and patient's anatomy were all aligned for obtaining additional images of the colon. Again the patient is turned into different positions so as to better demonstrate all of the specified areas of the abdomen prior to exposure. Sally then exited the exam room to develop the films and check them for image quality.

Morty waited in the room with Walter, who began to squirm and fidget with signs of obvious discomfort.

"Are we done here, kid?"

"I think so." Morty answered. "We just need to make sure the films are good before we drain the water out of you, and get you into the rest room." Time seemed to pass slowly, and Morty peered out of the doorway multiple times to see if Sally was on her way back to the room.

"Hey, kid, come over here." Walter called out, as he motioned for Morty's return to the exam table. At arm's length, the young man moved closer to the now agitated older man. "Hey, kid, do me a favor; take this thing out of my ass!"

Morty could not help but smile from the blunt nature of the request. "I wish that I could, sir, but we have to wait for Sally to tell us that we have finished the exam. Hang in there just a couple more minutes." The old man couldn't wait any longer for relief.

"Look, kid, I've spent a lot of time waiting on other people, and I'm done waiting. I only got so much time left on this earth, and I won't be spending another second of it with this tube up my ass."

With that said, he sat up on the table, reached his right hand around his back, and pulled the tube out from his rectum. A muffled moan accompanied the act as the still inflated balloon was expressed. Instantly, barium began to flow out of the patient's body, all while the discarded tubing allowed a constant stream from the opened clamp to begin flooding the table. Walter sat up, stepped down from the equipment, and walked straight toward the lavatory. A streaming white liquid trail of fluid followed. Morty moved quickly to clamp the line of the enema bag and contain the remaining liquid. He disposed of the enema supplies into a bio-hazardous waste receptacle, as fluid continued to coat the surrounding floor, walls, and equipment. Sally returned with a pleasant tone in her voice.

100

"OK, Mr. Sunderland, we're all done and you did great!" She paused to look around in shock at the enormous mess. "Where is Mr. Sunderland?" Morty moved with haste to apply towels to the areas in the most need of attention.

"He decided that he had waited long enough and then removed the tube from his body. After that, he walked into the restroom. I've been trying to clean up ever since." Sally approached the restroom and lightly knocked on the door.

"Mr. Sunderland, are you alright? Mr. Sunderland..." When he opened the door, she saw his gown was covered with barium, as was most of the toilet and floor.

"Are we finished here? I think I've had about enough for today." He then entered the exam room and lifted the bag of clothes and made his way toward the exit door. The soiled gown was completely open in the back, showing his exposed buttocks and legs that were coated with a white milky sheen.

"Morty, grab some towels and return him to the restroom for more attention. When you have finished in there, get back here and clean this room. When you're done with all of that, you can go to lunch." Sally turned and departed the room. Morty caught up with the elderly gentleman, and the pair returned to the lavatory. With extra towels, Morty did his best to sanitize the patient, and then helped to get him dressed. The elderly gentleman was finally escorted back to the waiting room where his daughter sat patiently.

"Did everything go alright?" She stood up and reached out to take his hand and move toward the exit.

"They did things to me that are against the Bible! Why in heaven's name did you bring me here?" Other patients witnessed the outburst, but remained quiet or stoic. He then pointed at Morty. "This guy here shoved a tube up my ass and filled me up like a water bed!"

Morty's response was his defense. "Now, technically, it was the radiologist that filled you up, and that's only because your doctor asked him, too." Walter was not amused.

"That's the last time I let you take me out for the day!" He spoke loud enough to attract everyone's attention in the room. Morty escorted them to the door.

"Thank you for choosing Our Lady of Miraculous Recovery," Morty said, as he waved to the couple during their departure. "We hope this test brings to you excellent results!" He returned to the exam room after gathering a considerable number of towels from the linen cart to aid in removing the remaining barium from the surrounding surfaces.

After the job was completed by wiping down all areas with an antiseptic solution, he removed the remaining splattered spots from his shoes, and then thoroughly washed his hands before leaving for lunch, and maybe a moment to relax. With only a couple of bites into his food, thoughts of Sarah began to fill his head.

Morty, can you hear me! He stopped chewing and swallowed his food.

I hear you, Sarah. What's up? He thought. She was frantic, and her words sounded desperate.

Morty, I'm late. It took a moment to produce a response.

Don't worry. Tomorrow, just wake up a little bit earlier in the morning and you'll be fine. He then took another bite of his food and resumed eating. *It's Monday; these things happen. You know, we had a very busy weekend.* She repeated her statement again, this time slowly and deliberately.

No, Morty, I'm late. I'm late for my period, and I'm scared. I need you here, right now. The food was placed back down on the tray, and all that was in his mouth was chewed and swallowed carefully.

Simmer down, now. You know I can't leave right now, or I'll get into a lot of trouble. I'll come straight over to your house after I have finished here at the clinic. Just try to relax. I'll be with you as soon as I can.

His appetite vanished, and silent reflection consumed all the remaining time of his lunch break. With such a distraction weighing so heavily on his mind, Morty managed to soldier through with the rest of the day, with very little attention or focus given to any task at hand. At four o'clock, he gathered his things and departed the hospital. He then drove straight over to Sarah's house.

She gazed out of the kitchen window in anticipation until Morty arrived. There, next to the curb, he was greeted with a passionate embrace just as he exited the car. Forcefully, she pulled him into the house and closed the door. Another kiss followed once safely inside. It seemed to calm her anxieties for a moment, and allowed her to speak coherently. "I thought you would never get here. What took you so long?"

"Well, I can only drive so fast, and there are other people on the road, and traffic lights, and stop signs…"

"OK, OK, I get it. Morty what are we going to do if I'm pregnant?" She began to weep softly. "How will I explain this to my parents?"

Morty gave the situation some serious thought and then answered. "We'll just tell them the truth. We were abducted by aliens from outer space, and forced to have sex on board their spaceship. We were powerless to stop them." The crying abruptly halted and she glared at him. He then tried to persuade a smile. "Don't worry. First off, you just started taking birth control pills. I've heard that can interfere with your menstrual cycle, until your body becomes adjusted. Second, we're going to be alright. And if it's true, then the baby is going to be alright, as well. Everything is going to be alright." A reassuring gaze into her eyes followed his words. "By the time our baby is born, I'll be done with school. I'll get a job and we'll get married and everything is going to be fine." She couldn't help but cry, but it wasn't a hysterical outburst.

"Promise me Morty: promise me we'll be alright. Tell me you'll be with me through everything."

"Of course, I will. We found our way into this together and we'll get through it together. Are you sure you're pregnant?"

"Well, no, but I'm sure that I'm scared." He held her a little closer.

"There's no need to be scared, just try to relax. When do you want to tell our parents?"

"I want to wait until the day of the baby shower, in eight and a half months when I'm totally showing." They both managed a restrained laugh.

"I can't see us waiting that long. Everything will happen in due time. I'll go home and check in with my parents and give you a call a little later. Are you going to be alright?"

"Yea, I think so. Go home and check on your mom. She's probably still upset about your brother." After sharing a reassuring embrace, they indulged in one more kiss before he departed for home.

Ethyl sat quietly in the living room while the television set aired the evening newscast. Knitting needles, along with skeins of blue and pink yarn lay atop the coffee table, as she busied herself creating multiple small knit caps.

"Hey, mom. How are you feeling today?" He leaned toward her for a kiss on the cheek.

"Alright, I guess." A long drawn out sigh escaped slowly from her body.

"What are you doing?"

"What does it look like I'm doing? I'm knitting. These little caps are for the newborn babies at the hospital, to keep their precious little heads warm." Her task continued for just a moment longer, then suddenly stopped. Silent tears streamed down her face, and after a moment she began to sob. Morty moved close to her in an attempt to offer consolation. "I'm sorry, honey. There's no reason for me to cry. I'm just not sure what I'm feeling right now."

"Don't worry about it, Mom. Everything is going to be fine." They hugged until comfort returned, and the knitting resumed. Morty excused himself to study schoolwork in his room. Demanding days brought with them exhaustion, so much that a short respite was necessary in the form of a nap before dinner, when Bart would return home from work.

10

Supper Man

Ethyl prepared a nice meal for the family to enjoy as the three sat quietly together at the dining room table. Hearty portions of food were dispensed onto each plate without the benefit of conversation until Morty broke the silence.

"This all looks delicious, Mom. Thank you so much." She acknowledged the compliment with a smile from across the table.

"You're welcome, sweetheart. There's plenty here, so, eat up." The clanking of utensils against dinner plates substituted for the sounds of conversation, until Bart chimed in with kudos for the wonderful flavor of the meal. Each member of the party in turn discussed the events of their respective days. Morty was careful not to divulge too much detail in regards to the catastrophic enema at the hospital, but still managed to make the story entertaining.

Ethyl shared with all her desire to resume a commitment as a volunteer at the hospital. This time it would be a little different, for now she wished to concentrate her energies on the newborn babies in the nursery. That was the reasoning behind the knitted caps that she created, and she expressed a desire to bath and change the babies, as well. A blissful tone returned to her voice as she spoke, as did the obvious upward swing in her demeanor. Bart reached over to take hold of her hand as she continued, and smiled with a show of support for the new endeavor. Once she finished speaking, Bart recounted his day at the office in a boring sort of way, as if he were reading a set of instructions for setting the electronic time display on any home appliance. As the interest of his audience seemed to wane, he changed the subject.

"Morty, this weekend I'm taking your mother to the coast. I've made reservations at the Paradise Inn Resort. We will be leaving here on Friday afternoon, and won't be home when you return from school. You'll have to take care of yourself. I thought that a nice long stay by the ocean was in order for your mother and me. I'll leave you some money for watching the house, but make sure you lock all the doors and windows before you leave for work or school." The unexpected news caught Ethyl by surprise and made her very happy.

"Oh, honey, this is exactly what I need. Thank you, so much!" She stood from her chair to lean over the table and give Bart a hug along with a kiss on his cheek. "I know it's only Monday, but I'm going to start packing our suitcases today for our trip!"

At the end of the meal, plates and utensils were collected from the table and carried to the kitchen sink. All the left-over food was packaged for storage, and placed in the refrigerator. Morty reset the table, as Bart returned all of the condiments to their proper storage. Any remaining food from the plates was discarded into the garbage. There was a noticeable prance in Ethyl's step, as she moved down the hall and to the bedroom. Bart managed on final command before departing.

"Son, why don't you load the dishwasher. I'm going to help your mother pack." As Morty began the chore, he sent a few thoughts out to Sarah.

Sarah, my parents are leaving for the weekend. We'll have this whole place all to ourselves. There was no immediate response, so he continued on with his task until completion. Alone in his room as he concentrated on studies, Sarah's thoughts came rushing at him.

Are you kidding me? They'll be gone all weekend? Morty, this is fantastic! This is just what I need, what we need. When are they leaving?

Friday afternoon, before I get home from school. Why did it take so long for you to respond to me?

I was in the middle of dinner with my parents. It was all I could do to stay at the table. This is going to be so perfect! We'll tell my parents that we're going out on a date, but instead we can hang out at your house. I can't wait!

The anticipation for their weekend gave cause for both to feel quite excited, but there was much study to be done first. He bid Sarah a good night and turned his attention back to the textbooks.

Early Wednesday morning, the young couple traveled together to school. Radiology technology classes would keep him on campus for most of the day, while Sarah spent considerable time in the library, for a chance to complete the necessary research on a history report that was due in just one week. Their plan was to meet for lunch at the cafeteria. A table was chosen outside of the building, for the weather was quite comfortable during this time of season when summer turned to autumn.

"I'm really looking forward to Friday. I can't wait to show you what I bought at the boutique. I know you're going to love it!" Sarah smiled in a provocative way, prior to taking a bite of her food.

"I'm excited, as well. I'll come to your house to pick you up, then we'll drive back to my house. I'll park the car in the garage, in case your parents drive by to check on us. What movie should we use as a cover for our date?"

"I've been giving this some thought and have come up with a better plan. You're going to take me out to dinner, and then we're going to say that we're attending a party at the apartment of one of your college friends here in Mercy Gulch. This way, we can stay out late without needing to know the plot of some movie that we haven't yet seen. You just need to come up with a cover story about the party." At that time, as if on cue, Billy Saragosa approached the table and interrupted the conversation.

"Hey, Morty! What are you doing?" Morty paused for a moment to look down at his plate of food, and then look back at Billy. "Yea," Billy replied, "I guess that was a stupid question."

"There are no stupid questions, only stupid people asking questions." Pause was given for digestion. "To answer your question, I'm having lunch with Sarah." He gestured in her direction with his hand.

"Hi, Sarah. I'm Billy. I'm sure Morty has told you all about me." She looked at him through a blank stare.

"No, I'm sorry. Am I missing something?" She looked at Morty.

"Aren't you that girl, in the hot tub, at the party?" Now she glared at Morty, with a much more focused stare. "Oh, no. Now I remember, that was that fine chick we saw in the parking lot last spring." Morty shook his head in disbelief, and Sarah quietly set her utensils down near the plate of food. It took a moment for Billy to realize how uncomfortable that last statement had made everyone feel. "Not to say that you're not fine, because you are, you know. Morty, you are one lucky guy, to have such a pretty lunch date, that is, if this is a date, or something." Billy's comments had dug such a deep hole that Morty now felt compelled to try and bury the conversation.

"OK, Billy, thanks for stopping by. I'll be seeing you soon, back in the classroom, after the break." He then motioned for Billy to leave.

"Anyway, it was nice to meet you, Sarah. I'll see you later, in class, Morty." He started to walk away, then stopped to turn back and address the couple. "I almost forgot to tell you, my parents are out of town this weekend, so I'm having a small party, on Friday. You can bring your friend, too." With a smile, he waved his hand, and continued on his way toward the classroom.

Morty felt compelled to apologize to Sarah regarding Billy's behavior. "I'm sorry about that. He doesn't mean any harm. Sometimes, he just talks without thinking first." He reached across the table to take a hold of her hand.

"When did you plan on telling me about the hot tub girl?" Sarah asked.

"Never, actually. Let me just say that, whatever has happened in the past, is just that, the past. That was a long time ago, before we ever became so close. You are the only girl in my life, and I won't do anything to hurt you, or us." He squeezed her hand a little tighter.

"I know you won't. I trust you, Morty. And besides, if you do screw this up, I promise I will make your life a living hell." A devious smile came over her lips. "At least now, we have the perfect cover story for this weekend. I need to get back to my history report. I'll see you later this afternoon." She stood up from the table, and moved around to give him a quick kiss good-bye.

"Yea, I need to get back to class as well. I'll walk with you back to the library." They gathered the school supplies and disposed of the trash from their lunch. With both backpacks slung over his shoulder, they walked while holding hands to the library. Morty made it a point to thank Billy in a rather sarcastic way, for the unsolicited visit during the lunch break.

Morty drove Sarah home after school, and that is where they found Lucille and Ethyl, enjoying an afternoon tea at the dining room table. All conversation between the two mothers halted abruptly as the young couple entered the house. The children dispensed with the expected gratuitous hugs to the mothers, as they remained seated at the table. Lucille then rose from her chair in declaration.

"I'm glad you're both here. We were just wondering what the two of you might have planned for this weekend?" The question caught them both by surprise.

"Not much," replied Sarah. "We both have to work. Is there something you need us to do?"

"No, just that Morty's parents will be out of town, so I just thought we could invite him over for dinner, on Friday." There was a distinct pause before Sarah responded with great enthusiasm.

"That sounds great! I'm sure Morty won't mind having a home cooked meal before we go out on our date." He was just a little slower to respond.

"Yea, that is very kind of you, Mrs. Fink. I would love nothing more than to join your family for dinner. My plan was to take Sarah out for a meal, but this sounds nice, too. Later that evening, a friend of mine is having a small get-together for his birthday. I thought we could stop by and drop off a card for him. We won't stay out too late. I'm sure we'll be home before midnight." Sarah slowly let out her breath.

"That all sounds wonderful! Thank you, Lucille, for such a thoughtful gesture. That will make me feel so much better about going out of town," replied Ethyl.

"I'll make sure that he takes home any leftover food. That should carry him over until you get back from your trip," added Lucille.

"Well, then, it's settled. Dinner with the Fink's on Friday. It's a date." Morty thanked Mrs. Fink for her hospitality, and excused himself to leave. Sarah walked him out to his car to bid him a proper good-bye. Billy's party idea was a blessing, and for just a moment, the earlier intrusion by his classmate was very much appreciated.

It seemed to take Friday morning forever to arrive. The alarm clock rang with the confirmation. As the started in the shower for Morty, the muffled sounds of his parents were heard through the wall as they prepared to leave for their trip. Down the hallway, Ethyl fussed over last minute details causing Bart to reply with a continuous stream of reassurances aimed to calm her anxieties. Soon the wheeled luggage clanked along the wooden floor down the hallway ending at the front door. Morty emerged from the bathroom just in time to bid them farewell.

"Alright, Son, I think we have everything. Your mother and I will be leaving shortly. Make sure you lock the doors and turn off any appliances before you leave the house. Don't bring anyone in, and don't leave the garage door open. Make sure you bring in the paper every morning, and leave the porch light on every night. The telephone number for the hotel is on the table by the phone. Remember, we trust you, so try not to do anything stupid." Bart counted on his fingers as he spoke, and seemed to cover everything to his satisfaction. With that, he opened the front door, and pulled the luggage outside to the car. "And tell your mother to hurry up. I don't want to get caught in a lot of traffic." The excitement was building within Morty, and he relayed his father's request for his mother's prompt departure. Bart sat in the car as it idled in the driveway. Ethyl gave Morty her final instructions.

"Now, I left food for you in the refrigerator, along with money in the cookie jar. If you need more than fifty dollars, you're out of luck. Lucille will drive by at different times to check on the house, so don't get any ideas about having any company over here. Make sure you lock the doors and…"

"OK, I get it. I just had this conversation with Dad. He wants you to get going, now! Go, and have a good time, and please don't worry about this place. Everything is going to be just fine." He escorted her out of the house, and walked her over to the car in the driveway. With one more kiss to the cheek, Morty aided in her departure, as he securely closed the passenger door of the car. They all waved good-bye until the parents drove around the corner, and vanished from sight.

Again, the clock on the wall could not move fast enough for Morty's liking. He practically ran out of the hospital once his shift had ended at four o'clock, and drove with abandon all the way home. Once there, he began to prepare the house for the anticipated evening events by straightening his room prior to Sarah's arrival.

Multiple candles had been carefully placed within selected rooms, to be lit at a later time, and create a more romantic ambiance. A deliberately laced scent of cologne

112

discreetly emanated from the bedding in his room, as a result of a light sprinkling to the pillows and comforter. Tonight would finally culminate in all that they had longingly anticipated since their somewhat out-of-body experience aboard the alien spacecraft. Now he would lovingly and delicately take Sarah, with her blessing, to bring completion to the deed started on that unpaved road near the creek. Risk was relatively high, but so was the ultimate reward of her body, mind, and soul, all hanging in the balance. Excitement now mounted exponentially, as the movement of the clock seemed to accelerate, and soon he would find himself at Sarah's house, sitting at the table for dinner with her family.

Instantly the door flew open upon Morty's arrival, as Sarah greeted him with much enthusiasm. Wearing a beautiful coral red dress, accented with sheer floral lace. She welcomed her gentleman caller with a discrete display of affection prior to her mother's appearance, and whisked him into the house. Under Ethyl's coaching, Morty presented fresh cut flowers to both ladies as he entered. Lucille hugged and then thanked him before placing the humble floral arrangements into a vase filled with water.

Ted soon entered the room and reached out to formally greet their guest. The two men shook hands before they moved to the den for some light conversation prior to the meal. The women busied themselves with final preparations for supper in the kitchen.

"Morty, how is everything going for you?"

"It's going great. I have just over a year remaining before graduation. My grades are holding up well, so I don't anticipate any problems. I have a part time job at the winery, to make a little extra money." Sarah peeked into the room to offer drinks, for which they were thankful.

"I'm glad to hear that things are going so well." There was a slight hesitation before he continued. "I also see that things are going well for my daughter. You know, Morty, Sarah means the world to us, and we only want what is best for her.

You are a nice young man, and we have grown very fond of you, and your family, and hold all of you in the highest regard." Morty sat on the edge of the sofa cushion as Ted spoke with calculated caution. "What I'm trying to say is, don't hurt my little girl. She means everything to me. Someday, if you are lucky enough, you too will have a little girl of your own to love and protect, and only then will you will understand." Morty seized the opportunity to interrupt the speech.

"I understand right now, Mr. Fink. I assure you, I have only the best of intentions for Sarah. I think the world of her, and would never do anything to hurt her. You can believe in me, sir." Ted managed a smile, which allowed Morty to relax back into the seat, just a little bit. Sarah returned to the room and announced that the food had been served. The men adjourned to the dining room and took their seats at the table.

Morty found the meal to be enjoyable, although still lacking much of an appetite. He managed to eat all that was on his plate. Talk at the table consisted of topics pertaining to the weather and such innocuous subjects. His excitement mounted, and became more difficult to mask within his best behavior. Such was prominently displayed for the benefit of all, but nervously found his date to show a little less reserve. Somewhere, she found the audacity to act with sass while responding to the most routine questions from her parents. Morty attempted to rein her in using a light tap of his foot to her ankle under the table.

After such a hearty meal, Lucille excused herself to generously prepare food for Morty to take home. The young couple collected up all the dishes from the table. Sarah rinsed the food from the plates as Morty loaded the dishwasher.

Lucille then placed the bouquet of fresh flowers at the center of the table, and stopped for just a moment to admire them. Sarah gave her father a hug and kiss in the den, then helped Morty carry the food, all while bidding farewell to her parents. They were quizzed once more by Lucille in regards to every detail of their plan for the evening as they departed the house. With a distinct accelerated pace, Sarah addressed all her concerns, kissed her mother good-bye, and escorted her date out to the car.

Sarah proved to be quite giddy, and found it difficult to contain her enthusiasm. Everything was funny or especially beautiful and cute. Morty's nervousness surfaced, and he stuttered a bit with speech. They both dreamed of this day, and their fate awaited, but neither could know how it would all play out. She wondered out loud about the preparations for the special night, and his voice crackled with each response.

They pulled into the driveway and Morty set the transmission to the 'P' position. He then bolted through the gate that lead to the back yard and entered the garage through the side access. The large electric door opened, and the car was moved inside before the engine stopped. The two looked at each other and smiled. The large garage door closed before they entered into the house. Once safely across the threshold, they now passed the point of no return.

11

Wake me when it's Over

Progression through the house was abruptly halted as they reached the kitchen, but only long enough for Morty to light the candles he had placed earlier that day. A soft, flickering glow of lights lined a path through the hallway that culminated at the entrance to his bedroom. It became more difficult for Sarah to corral her enthusiasm as she neared the door with a hastened pace. There, at the gateway to all things anticipated, Morty slowly pushed the door open, and released the musk-laced fragrance set previously intended to add a touch of masculinity to the otherwise heavily juvenile décor. As they crossed through the doorway, a cassette tape machine on the nightstand was activated to fill the air with soft, romantic music meant to enhance the experience.

The blinds were drawn closed to aid in masking the numerous model airplanes and comic books dispersed throughout the room. Morty quietly closed the door before lighting even more candles to create a desired atmosphere for romance. Sarah showed her appreciation for his effort with an expression of awe, as she slowly scanned around the room, and savored every moment.

"Well, what do you think?" Morty asked, with a tone that carried an air of pride in accomplishment, with just a hint of fear, all at the same time.

"I think this is the most beautiful room I have ever seen." With her gazing green eyes locked onto his, they embraced. Slow, wet, deep kisses followed, along with the fluid motion of his hands as they grasped tightly at her hips and waist. He pulled her closer, and Sarah offered no resistance, with her arms wrapped firmly around his neck and their eyes closed.

The pull tab of the dress' zipper offered little resistance, and succumbed to the gentle tug from the tips of his fingers. Slowly down the entire of her back, the fabric split along the teeth of the tape. She lowered her arms, allowing the garment to easily slide down her torso and drop silently to the ground. For just one fleeting moment she stood statuesque, wearing only her most delicate of unmentionables, when he paused for brief reflection. That moment quickly passed in as much time as it took to step out of the pile of clothing that now lay on the carpeted floor.

Sarah then took charge, and began to pull Morty's shirt from out from under the waistband of his pants, and didn't stop until it was fully removed and discarded atop her dress. The pants were next to go, unbuttoned and lowered, as he kicked his way out of his shoes. With boxer's type undershorts, and plain white athletic socks that clung to the level of his upper calves, Morty looked more like a fighter, minus the gloves, before entering the ring.

Kissing resumed and intensified, along with a progressive mutual exploration with their hands of the inexperienced but zealous participants. Morty fumbled horribly as he tried to unclasp the simple hooks that held her brazier tightly closed. Recognizing his struggle, she effortlessly reached behind her back and released the garment. He then gently eased her down onto the mattress of the bed. Her panties were the last piece of clothing to remain, but not for long, for now all of their pubescent fears were melting away, and Morty now felt he was in total control. The satin swath of cloth stood no chance as he slid them off her hips and completely down to her delicate ankles. With a simple kick of her foot, they flew high into the air and landed on top of the Morty's clothes dresser.

There she lay completely defenseless, without reservations, in all her naked glory. This fact was not lost on Morty, as all of his emotions and anticipation for such intimacy rose up, a sight made obvious by the rapidly increasing size of his manhood.

No words were shared or needed to be, as the expression on Sarah's face spoke volumes. She could not stop staring at him, nor he at her, as the pillowed comforter atop the bed was pulled back to give invitation to the sheets below. Those same shared smiles were indelible as the pair submerged themselves between the linens and resumed what would surely be the most unforgettable experience of their young lives. Things then came to an abrupt halt.

"Sarah, I don't know if I can do this."

"What are you talking about?" She answered with total confusion. "You look pretty ready to me."

"It's not that. Today, your dad sat me down for a talk in the den. He got me thinking about, like, what if you were my little girl?"

Don't even go there," she replied with a most annoyed tone. "I don't care if you spoke to Mahatma Gandhi in one of your dreams. I have patiently waited for what seems an eternity for tonight, and so have you. We know in our hearts that this is right, and the timing is perfect. We are in this thing too deep, and I will not entertain any ideas about turning back now. We are both adults. You just stay focused and do what you came here to do, mister." Her enthusiasm was breathtaking, as well as quite convincing.

"I'm sorry, you're right. I just thought I needed say something."

"Well then, very good. I have taken note of your concerns. Now, I must insist that you shut the fuck up and get busy." Sarah then reached for the small handbag that she so carefully accessorized to her outfit. The purse was opened and a chain of four unsealed condoms was removed. One was detached from the links and handed to Morty.

"I think you should retire the old one that you've been carrying in your wallet all this time. There's probably an expiration date on those kind of things." With this being his first time using such an apparatus, there was a slight delay in the proceedings until Morty could remove it from the wrapper and place it appropriately onto his person. A small, squeezable tube was also been produced from the purse. Sarah removed the top and took a moment to read the directions on the package. She then applied a clear gelatinous substance to her genitalia. "It's a little bit of lubricant with spermicide. All this should keep us safe, but just to be sure, don't finish your business inside of me."

With all the preparations now complete, he positioned himself on top of her and slowly eased his way inside her body. Initially his motions were slow and careful before the pace of his movements increased. She grimaced slightly at first, but soon found a heightened level of comfort with the speed and depth of his efforts. A tantric level of awareness followed, whereas Sarah released all chastity along with any notion of resistance, and allowed herself to truly feel the ecstasy of the act. Waves of quiet moaning emanated during this state of enchantment.

Morty by comparison, began a strenuous work out. Motivation came from a story that was told many times during his youth: A small locomotive faced with a daunting, uphill task.

Mentally he began to chant, *I think I can, I think I can, I think I can.*

To which Sarah responded, *I know you can, I know you can, I know you can.*

Much like an appliance of convenience, he worked with persistent regularity and purpose. It was as if he were controlled by some external force, with the sole purpose of performing this specific task: to stimulate all of her sensory receptors through tenacious fornication. This instinctive effort subjugated any lingering doubts as to the depth of their feelings for each other. Feelings that would be forever remembered in the beautiful sounds of her exultation produced with increased frequency and volume. With one final moan, her senses exploded with a release of energy unlike any felt before, and she quietly wept. Those delicately manicured fingernails clung tightly to the skin of his back, and then waned through a slowly loosened grip. Morty soon achieved his climax as well, and was quick to extract

119

himself from her tight hold, and made sure to express his seed into the prophylactic sheath safely outside of her body. Morty then collapsed next to her on the bed to enjoy the pleasurable mix of euphoria and mild exhaustion relevant to the act. He turned to her and lightly kissed her lips. It was then Morty noticed the tracks from her tears as they rolled down her face.

"I'm sorry, did I hurt you? Did I do it wrong?" He asked. "I was afraid I would screw this up."

"No, you idiot. You did it just right. That was beautiful." More tears began to stream from her eyes and down her cheeks, until they were wiped away by the soft touch of his hand. "That was everything I hoped it would be." Those words brought with them the realization to the single most wonderful experience of his young life; much better than any nocturnal emissions during his wildest dreams, or previously self-induced orgasms through manual manipulation.

"Me too! We should have started doing this a long time ago." Smiles overcame the faces of the young lovers, all which was suddenly lost when the bedroom door opened most unexpectedly. Captured completely by surprise, Morty pulled up on the bed covers to shield Sarah from the eyes of the intruder, but all was for naught. There would be no escape, as they had been caught literally with their pants down. Resorting to tactics from her youth, Sarah closed her eyes tightly and cringed in a futile attempt at hiding, while Morty's eyes, in contrast, remained wide open.

There in the doorway stood Sheldon, who seemed just as surprised as the compromised couple.

"Sheldon, what are you doing here?" Morty barked with anger.

"I should be asking you that same question. I just came home to see Mom and Dad, but I never expected to see this!" Sarah forced open her eyes and quickly glanced at Morty's brother.

"Sarah Fink, is that you? My how you've grown, and into such a beautiful young lady, as well. Do all of our parents know about this little soiree?"

"Sarah and I have been dating for nearly a year now, so yes they know that much," replied Morty. As far as us being naked in my bed, well, no, that much they don't know, and we would appreciate that it remains that way." Sheldon could not help but to glean the humor of this unforeseen turn of events, and indulged himself with a continued interrogation.

"I didn't see your car in the driveway, little brother, so I didn't think anyone was home. Oh, and by the way, I extinguished those candles you left in the kitchen, so you wouldn't burn the whole house down." The pair began to shuffle beneath the bedding for privacy as Morty reached for the pile of clothes and pulled them under the blanket. "Are you two about done here, or should I come back in a little bit?" Morty then tossed one of his shoes directly at Sheldon.

"Yea, you're about done here, so kindly get the hell out of my room, and close the door!" With joyful hesitation, Sheldon complied by slowly shutting the bedroom door as he departed.

"That was so embarrassing," Sarah stated. Next time, we need to lock that door." Just then, the doorbell rang. The pair instantly froze and held their breaths. Sheldon was soon heard to greet the uninvited guest at the porch.

"Mrs. Fink, what a pleasant surprise. I'm afraid my parents aren't here right now, and I'm not quite sure when they will return."

"Oh, Sheldon, this is a surprise. Your parents are away for the weekend. I saw lights on in the house, as I was driving by, so I stopped in for a look. I promised your folks I would keep an eye on the place while they're gone." She noticed the candles placed along the countertops. "What's with all the candles?"

"Well, when I first came in, the lights didn't seem to be working, so I lit these candles. I later found that the electrical breaker in the panel had tripped, so I reset it. Everything seems to be working fine now." He smiled as he replied. "You don't happen to know where my brother is, do you."

"Well, as a matter of fact, I do. It seems, in your absence at school, your brother and my daughter have become quite fond of each other. They are out on a date at this very minute."

"You don't say, well that's quite the news. I had no idea the two had become so fond of each other. How old is Sarah now?" Sheldon rubbed his chin as he spoke.

"She's eighteen. Can you believe it?"

"Oh, my goodness, where does the time go? Why it seems like just yesterday those two were running around the yard, playing simple games and having the time of their young lives. They grow up so darn fast."

"That they do, Sheldon." She crinkled her nose and took a step back. "What on earth is that smell?" Sheldon also noticed the odor and responded.

"Oh that. Well, when the lights went out, I spilled a whole bottle of cologne in the bathroom. I'm afraid the house will be smelling of musk for quite some time." They smiled at each other cordially.

"Well anyway, it was nice to see you again, Sheldon. The phone number to the hotel where your parents are staying should be right next to the phone, and there's food in the refrigerator. If you need anything just call us."

"Thank you so much, Mrs. Fink. That is very kind of you. Have a great weekend, and I'm sure I'll be seeing you again soon. Give my best to your husband." He waved as she retreated down the driveway, and made her way back towards her home. Sheldon then closed the front door.

Morty and Sarah sat rigid with fear, and did not move or speak the entire time her mother was addressing Sheldon. He soon found the courage to peak through the slightly opened blinds to confirm that Lucille was indeed moving away from the house. He motioned with his hand to Sarah that her mother was gone from view, to which she let out a sigh of relief. Moments later, there was a light tapping at the bedroom door.

"I think the coast is clear," announced Sheldon's muffled voice through the door. You two might want to think about rapping up this part of your date. I realize that a little excitement should be anticipated, but this is a bit more than either of you bargained for, don't you think?"

"Thanks, Sheldon," Morty called back, "I think you may be right. The moment had passed and it was now time to remove the used prophylactic. In an attempt at humor, he displayed it to Sarah prominently between his fingers. Pride was on display, however ill-advised, during that moment of hesitation while deciding how to dispose of it.

"Don't be gross, Morty. I think we're done with that." She acknowledged his accomplishment with a gentle kiss. The bed covers were drawn down as she stood up. That's when she noticed something horrible.

"Oh my God, Morty, look!" Sarah pointed at the bed. There in the middle of the mattress was a huge red spot in the center of the sheet. "You started my period." They both stared in quiet disbelief. The bright red blood stain covered an area about the size of a typical salad plate.

"Are you sure?" Never before had his ignorance been exhibited so prominently.

"Well, this isn't the first time that I've experienced bleeding from my mama part, and the pelvic cramping may have had something to do with it. What are we going to do now?" Morty dressed in his clothes while Sarah began to collect her garments. All of the bedding was removed to better evaluate the upper surface area of the mattress. Morty then gathered up all the sheets for cleaning. Sarah was now completely dressed, but chose to forgo her panties until an opportunity presented to tend to the 'mama part' a bit better.

"Do you have a tampon?" She asked.

"Not on me, but I'm pretty sure my mom must have something like that around here somewhere. Why don't you check inside her bathroom while I get started on cleaning up?" She kissed him gently before leaving the room to walk down the hall. Morty passed by his brother who stood in the kitchen. The linen was taken to the garage for cleaning as Sheldon prepared a snack from the leftovers found in the refrigerator. He inquired as to his brother's intentions with the linen.

"What in the world do you have there?" The soiled sheet was splayed just enough to discretely show the area of concern. "Whoa, little man, I think you popped her cherry! What a stud you turned out to be. You know that stain is never coming out of that sheet." Morty stopped for a moment and sighed after hearing the disappointing news.

"What am I going to do before Mom and Dad get home?" Sheldon thought for a moment before offering a solution to the problem.

"If I were you, I would dump a whole jar of salsa on the stain and let it soak in. When Mom gets home, tell her you were eating in your room and spilled it on your bed. Just make sure there's still plenty of salsa left on the sheet, you know, chunks of peppers, tomatoes and whatnot. That should be enough to cover your tracks.

"Why was I eating in my room?"

"I don't know. Maybe, because you're an idiot? Look, I don't have all of the answers. You'll have to do some thinking for yourself." Sheldon returned to the preparation of his food as Morty opened the door to remove a jar of salsa from the refrigerator.

"Hey, Sheldon, I was just wondering, how are you doing?" There was a pause for reflection before he answered.

"Well, OK, I guess. It's weird: for a long time I have waited for this day to come. I've been carrying this burden for a better part of my adulthood, and now it has finally been lifted from my shoulders. I know, I should feel very happy, but I don't. I've always known this about myself, so there's really no change to my feelings personally, but I know this has upset the folks, and for that I am truly sorry. It was never my intention to hurt anyone; I only want to be me." A slight smile crossed over his lips. "And judging by what I saw earlier tonight, they don't need to worry much about future grandchildren." Sheldon then mussed Morty's hair with a friendly swipe of his hand.

Sarah was now dressed, and joined the two brothers in the kitchen. "Well, hello Miss Sarah Fink. It's so nice to see you, oh, wait a minute, I think I've seen more of you tonight then I ever would have expected." She turned her head away for a moment in shame, then allowed herself a smile of sinful delight.

"Sheldon, Morty told me about what has been happening with you. I hope you don't mind me asking, but, what makes you feel the way you do, you know, about sex?" Sheldon took a moment for reflection before responding with a slight tone of humor to his voice.

"Honey, after what I saw you doing to my brother in his bed, you're probably the one person that wouldn't need me to explain myself, or my feelings. We seem to have more in common than you might realize." Morty interrupted the conversation with a question of his own.

"Is there someone special in your life right now?"

"Yea, that's part of the problem." Sheldon spoke slowly to avoid confusion or misunderstanding. "His name is Chet, and I met him at school. We've been seeing each other for the better part of a year. Mom and Dad want me to come home for Thanksgiving, and I want Chet to come, as well. I thought about lying in regards to our relationship, but I don't want to lie anymore. I know it may be painful for them, but I need to be true to myself." Morty smiled in agreement.

"Well, you know, this may mean the end of your favorite son-run that you've enjoyed all these years," Morty stated.

"Are you kidding me? I'm not the favorite son!" replied Sheldon. "They are always bragging about you. And this little liaison between the two of you should pretty much cement it all in your favor. I don't see how I could ever top that."

Morty embraced his brother in a sign of support, then excused himself to finish hiding any evidence of his brief dalliance. In the garage, Sarah joined him and helped with the staging of the salsa incident. Clean sheets from the cabinet were procured and the couple returned his room to a more presentable state. They took solace through reflection, and worked together quietly to complete the task. When the silence was broken, Sarah had a suggestion for the remainder of their evening.

"Maybe, when we're done here, we should go to that party your friend told us about at school."

"Yea, that sounds like a good idea. Let's finish up and get going." Soon they were ready to leave the house, so they returned to Morty's car, and backed it out of the garage. Sheldon waved, as they moved out to the driveway, then he closed the electric door as they drove away. Conversation was scarce between the two for the rest of the evening, but displays of affection were abundant. They seemed to bask in the afterglow of emotional and physical satisfaction, and found it impossible to stop smiling at each other for any length of time. After a brief visit to the party, they both agreed it was time to put an end to their evening, and he drove Sarah home. With one final kiss on the front porch, the young lovers parted company. Reflecting on the night, it had seemed nearly as perfect as possible, just like Morty always pictured it would be, or at least close enough.

12

Back to Basics

Morty awoke the next morning to the sound of the telephone ringing in the kitchen. He hurriedly jumped up from his bed, and ran down the hall to answer the call. His parents were still out of town, and he wanted to be sure they were doing fine. The receiver was raised; it was Sarah.

"I've been trying to contact you all morning with my thoughts. Why haven't you answered me?" A moment of pause was taken to gain perspective.

"Well, good morning to you, too. Sorry, I didn't hear you in my head. You just woke me up with the phone." She seemed quite perturbed with his response and a definite change could be detected in her voice.

"Wait a minute," she said. Morty stood silently holding the phone handset for nearly a full minute of silence before she returned. "Did you hear any of that?"

"Hear any of what?" There was another silence before she erupted.

"Damn it! It doesn't work anymore! How am I going to know what you're thinking?" The situation became more apparent, and solicited a chuckle with his amusement. "This isn't funny, not at all!" The next words from his mouth were chosen very carefully. Not an easy task, as he had yet to fully awaken to the day.

"Sweetheart, you don't need to read my mind to know what I'm thinking. I'm always thinking about you." The comment seemed prosed to provide calm at a vulnerable moment, but gave an assurance of promise nonetheless. A noticeable change in her attitude was apparent through a more angelic sound to her voice.

"Oh, Morty, you always know the right thing to say to me. Are your parents back at home yet?"

"No, I haven't heard from them. I don't expect they'll be home until sometime tomorrow. I hope they get home soon, so they get a chance to see Sheldon before he goes back to Capa City."

"Yea, that would be nice. What are you doing this morning?" Sarah's tone sounded a little more inviting.

"I was hoping you would come by and help me cut the yard. After that, we could clean up a little bit then go do your yard before you go to work." It only took a moment for her to respond.

"I have a better idea. Why don't I come over and we can continue what we started last night?" He hesitated for a moment before responding.

"But, I'm all out of salsa." She found no humor in his answer, but agreed it would be best to abstain from such relations for the day.

"Yea, you're probably right. I'm still coming over, so I'll be there soon." They exchanged amorous affirmations before the call ended, and Morty returned the handset back to the base of the phone. In the kitchen, a carton of milk was removed from the refrigerator, along with some of the leftover food from the night before. As Morty prepared a plate for breakfast, Sheldon emerged from his bedroom and greeted him through conversation.

"Good morning, Morty. How are you feeling today?" Morty thought about the question for a moment and smiled as he answered.

"Actually, I feel pretty darn good. How about you?" No sooner had he finished the sentence, a stranger entered the room, which caught Morty a little by surprise.

"Morty, this is Chet. He came down from Capa City last night." Morty reached out to shake his hand in greeting.

"Nice to meet you, Chet. Is this your first visit to Stillwater?"

"No, actually. I've been here in town before, but it is the first time that I've stayed here at the house."

"Welcome. I hear you will be back for Thanksgiving. That's a great time to visit, as well as Easter," Morty graciously stated. "Mom's a great cook, and I'm sure you'll enjoy it."

"I certainly hope so. Let's just see how things go before I start making any holiday reservations."

"Well, if you're not here, then I won't be here either," added Sheldon. "What are your plans for this morning, brother?"

"Sarah's coming over to help me with the yard. You know, if the two of you pitch in as well, this will go much faster."

"Well, Morty, sorry to disappoint but we need to get back to Capa City," answered Sheldon. They gathered up some food and retreated back to the bedroom to pack their belongings. Within a few minutes, Sarah had arrived, and Morty welcomed her into the house. After a delicate exchange of mutual admiration, they proceeded to the opened garage, and began gathering equipment necessary for tending to the lawn. Lucille stopped by at nearly the same time that the young couple had completed with the clipping of the grass in the front yard. She insisted that her intent was solely to invite Morty over for lunch at the house, but all could appreciate the motive behind her unannounced visit.

Once the gardening was complete, the pair retreated into the house for cool, liquid refreshment. Morty playfully tickled Sarah which prompted a joyful squeal. It was then Morty had a change of heart.

"What do you say we go to my room? I have a fresh set of sheets on the bed."

"You should have thought about that before we became covered in sweat and dust. Besides, I'm bleeding like a stuck pig, and we need to do my parent's yard before I go to work." He teased her again with more tickling, to which she weakly resisted, and then insisted that they get going to her house.

After all the landscaping jobs had been completed, the two washed their faces and hands, then joined her parents for brunch. Sarah would soon need to get ready for work, so the meal was a little hurried. Afterward, Morty was again sent on his way with a package of food, prepared by Lucille for him to enjoy later that evening while at work.

The two managed to shield themselves from the omnipotent watch of her parents just long enough to share an abbreviated exchange of salty affection at the front door. She gazed deeply at him, as if there was some burden that weighed heavily on her mind. It was hounding her and needed to be said out loud.

"Morty, I don't want to scare you, but there is something I have to tell you." She paused for just a moment. "I love you." He smiled, and basked for just a moment in the warmth of her statement.

"I love you, too." Again, they expressed their shared affections with a kiss. He soon departed her company and drove home, to allow her adequate opportunity to prepare for the upcoming work shift at the boutique.

His ride home was a short one, and once there he found Sheldon and Chet preparing for their return trip to Capa City. They traveled light by utilizing small canvas duffle bags as luggage, which they loaded into the back seat of Sheldon's car. Morty parked his car along the curb and approached his brother in the driveway.

"Alright, Sheldon, it was good to see you. Chet, it was nice to meet you, too. I hope you guys have a safe trip home, and I'm sure I'll be seeing you both very soon." He gave his brother a masculine hug, the kind generally shared between manly men, especially brothers.

"Thanks, Morty. It was good to see you, too. Good luck with Sarah, and tell Mom and Dad that I'm sorry I missed them. I'll give them a call later, after they get home from their trip."

Sheldon entered the car and closed the door. The window was then rolled down, as final farewells were expressed and the vehicle backed away from the house and departed. Morty went inside to begin his own preparations for work, starting with a much needed shower.

As he basked in the therapeutic effects of the cascading water, he reflected on the incredible events of the weekend, and how his feelings had so drastically matured within the short span of just a few days. Those feelings shared between he and Sarah had now risen to a new level, much to their satisfaction, and it was all good. No longer would there be a need to agonize over the unknown details of their first intimate encounter, or give any worry to Sarah's needs. Now his primary objective was to find ways to allow them to do it again, and again, and again, but to do it responsibly, and without getting caught. Thoughts of Sarah flooded his mind to an undeniable level; he was truly in love.

Once back in the bedroom, his pace was relaxed, as his work shift at the winery was still hours away. All within the house was quiet, and Morty took a moment to enjoy the peaceful serenity, and to meditate prior to the hustle of the day's events that would surely unfold.

When the towel used to dry his hair was removed from atop his head, he was startled to find the intergalactic aliens standing before him. "Both still wore the clothing taken from within Sarah's closet. They gestured to Morty, trying to gain his attention by waving all of their upper extremity-like hands. The surprise of their arrival caused him to jump backward, and land softly into a sitting position on top of the bed.

We do not intend to scare you; we mean you no harm Again, just as before, communication was carried out telepathically, with no verbal words spoken.

You guys need to quit sneaking up on me; it's incredibly rude. In no time, he was able to once again feel a level of comfort while interacting with the returning visitors.

We have come to bid you farewell, and to thank you for your help. The use of your carbon based fuels have provided us the means to return to our home, and the fertilized carbon-based zygote you provided will be of great assistance to the evolution of our species for millennia to come. Our hope is to infuse some of the more desirable elements of the human species genome into our own. Morty interrupted the transfer of thoughts for clarification.

What fertilized carbon-based zygote, I never provided you with anything. What are you referring to?

The seed which we removed from your female counterpart. If this is a problem, we can replant it into her body. He thought for just a moment before replying.

No, no, no, that won't be necessary. We're not ready for that yet, and you guys were responsible for that, not me. I brought protection.

Very well, then it is decided. You have proved to be a most valuable resource, and we would like to reciprocate in kind. We have isolated the mutant protein that has caused disruption of the formative molecules found within the affected creatures around the creek. We have developed an antidote and dispersed it into the environment. This will resolve any future problems, and bring an end to any further mutations. Is there anything else we can do for you? Morty thought for a moment before he answered.

You know that telepathy thing? Sarah was quite disappointed when we lost that ability. Is there any way we can get that back? The visitors looked at each other and seemed to communicate outside of Morty's comprehension. They turned their attention back to him with a response.

The more delicate, or in your case, feminine units of all species in the universe have always desired an ability to interpret the thoughts and feelings of their more masculine counterparts. This is true with my species, as well. If it is your wish, we can make this possible, but a word of warning, once it is done, it cannot be reversed. Morty again took a moment for reflection before responding.

On second thought, I don't think that will be necessary. Let's just keep that little nugget to ourselves. The alien visitors appeared to understand, as they both nodded their heads slowly.

Very good. Farewell, one called Morton Eaton Thorton, perhaps our paths will cross again at some point. Until then, peace and enlightenment to you.

Yea, yea, piece of a lightened mint to you, too. Now you guys need to get out of here. I have to get ready for work, and I can't afford to lose three hours today.

The interstellar travelers soon took their leave, and Morty returned to his task of preparing for work. A quick glance at the clock assured him that no unaccounted time had passed during their visit.

Portions of the generously donated food from the recent visits to the Fink's house were packed inside a paper bag before he departed for work. As he entered the winery grounds, Benny could be seen driving the shuttle truck through the gate with a loaded trailer of grapes for processing. The two friends greeted each other with a casual wave of the hand. Morty's car was then parked in the proper location near the security office. He carried the bag of food into the small building before placing it into the refrigerator. Sarge did not acknowledged his arrival, and continued with the usual task of directing traffic during the change of shift. After off-loading the trailer, Benny stopped his truck back at the gate to extend a more proper greeting to his good friend.

"¡Morty! ¿Que pasa, amigo? The magnitude of volume used to extend the salutation carried easily above the noise of the surrounding traffic. As he climbed down from the cab of the truck, a slowing of vehicular movement adjacent to the main entrance ensued. This fact was no lost on Sarge, who quickly moved to address the recurrent and deliberate cause behind the problem. Benny enthusiastically greeted his chum with a handshake at the doorway to the office. "What in this world is new with you?"

"The question is, what's not new with me?" Morty replied. A blinding smile of sheer bliss refused to be disguised, and piqued Benny's curiosity.

"Whatsoever do you refer to, young squire?" Sarge had arrived to the office, boiling with anger. He stood at the doorway with an undeniable air of authority, and ready for any confrontation.

"This truck must be moved immediately! You are in violation of traffic code number VC-420, parts a, b, and c, and therefore, this vehicle must be moved immediately!" Benny was taken aback by the rude nature of the interruption, and seized the opportunity to directly address the Sarge.

"Yea, yea, yea, go frisk yourself, Dick!" Morty suppressed his amusement, so as not to add more fuel to the fire which burned deep within Sarge's belly, and Benny seemed compelled to stoke.

"My name is Richard!" I'm putting you on report!" As he stormed away, he replaced the whistle to his mouth and began to blow near continuously, all while waving his hands at the collection of cars, ordering them through the intersection. Benny casually returned his attention back to Morty.

"So, where were we? Oh yes, now I remember; what in heaven's name are you talking about?" Again, it was impossible for Morty to mask his amusement, or pride in accomplishment, so he just came out with it.

"Sarah and I did it this weekend." He then waited for Benny's reaction.

"Does that mean what I think it means?" Morty nodded his head repeatedly. "Well, well, well, the squire is now the lord. Bless you, my son." He mussed the top of Morty's hair with his hand and smiled. "It's about time. I was beginning to think maybe you weren't into that sort of thing." An annoyed look replaced the earlier grin on Morty's face.

"I just wanted it to be right, to be perfect, that's all." With hesitation, Benny prodded.

"Well, was it?" Morty took a moment to choose his words carefully.

"Yes, yes it was."

"Why don't I believe you?" Benny replied.

"OK, OK, actually, we got caught by my brother, and that was after she left a big blood stain on my sheets; other than that, it was perfect." Their dialog was momentarily interrupted, as the two friends took notice of the frantic display outside from Sarge. They could clearly see through the window his apparent frustration through the spastic movements. "Aren't you worried that you'll get into trouble?" Morty asked.

"Naw, I aint too worried about that. Maybe he'll get me a suspension, and then I'll be forced to take a couple of days off." The two enjoyed a moment of levity before Benny returned to the cab of his truck. With a wave of the hand through the truck's window followed by a blast from the air horn that commanded everyone's attention, he drove away. Sarge appeared to settle down soon after Benny's departure, and true to his word, filed a lengthy and scathing report in the ledger with regards to the traffic incident. Morty took it all in stride, and as if on cue, Reña approached the gate, once again carrying a covered plate of food. Morty tried to thank her as best he could in her native Spanish language before he placed the food into the small refrigerator. The delicious aroma of the gift caused him to salivate, and look forward to a time when the activities at the gate would settled down and allow him an opportunity to enjoy such a gift.

Bart and Ethyl returned from their jaunt on Sunday with a refreshed attitude. Disappointed to discover that they had missed out on an opportunity to see Sheldon, they felt confident that he would return home soon to celebrate the holidays, and bring with him a chance for reconciliation and acceptance.

Although the house was in fine shape upon their arrival, the salsa story didn't seem to cut the mustard with Bart, but he managed to mask those concerns, for Ethyl's sake.

Morty and Sarah continued to grow as a couple. They began to plan for their future, with all of the joy and excitement that would come with it. It's not to say that there would be no issues or concerns, on the contrary, but they now enjoyed a special bond between them. Such would provide solace regardless of the challenge, even without the aid of telepathy. That would always be remembered with great fondness: The short period of time when their good fortune permitted such a unique gift to be shared. Alas, as Morty was prone to say to Sarah, "I still have a pretty good idea of what you're thinking, even if I you're not inside of my head."